I Don't Want To Die
A Love Story

by
James D. Shrum, Sr.

Cork Hill Press
Carmel

Cork Hill Press
597 Industrial Drive, Suite 110
Carmel, IN 46032-4207
1-866-688-BOOK
www.corkhillpress.com

Copyright © 2004 by James D. Shrum, Sr.

This book is a work of fiction. All the events, places and characters are products of the author's imagination or used fictitiously. Any resemblance to actual events or locales or persons, living or dead, is purely coincidental.

All rights reserved under International and Pan-American Copyright Conventions. With the exception of brief quotations in critical reviews or articles, no part of this work may be reproduced or transmitted in any form or by any means, electronic or mechanical, including photocopying, recording, or any information storage or retrieval system, without permission in writing from the publisher.

Trade Paperback Edition: 1-59408-127-1

Printed in the United States of America

1 3 5 7 9 10 8 6 4 2

Table of Contents
Part One — Eternal Rape

DEDICATION	v
CAST OF CHARACTERS	vii
FOREWORD	ix
BIOGRAPHY OF THE AUTHOR	xi
CHAPTER 1	1
CHAPTER 2	7
CHAPTER 3	10
CHAPTER 4	12
CHAPTER 5	18
CHAPTER 6	21
CHAPTER 7	24
CHAPTER 8	29
CHAPTER 9	33
CHAPTER 10	34
CHAPTER 11	36
CHAPTER 12	41
CHAPTER 13	45
CHAPTER 14	50
CHAPTER 15	55

Part Two—I Don't Want to Die

CHAPTER 1	63
CHAPTER 2	68
CHAPTER 3	72
CHAPTER 4	76
CHAPTER 5	79
CHAPTER 6	83
CHAPTER 7	86
CHAPTER 8	91
CHAPTER 9	95
CHAPTER 10	98
CHAPTER 11	102
CHAPTER 12	105
CHAPTER 13	109
CHAPTER 14	112
CHAPTER 15	116
BIBLIOGRAPHY	119

DEDICATION

This book is dedicated to my wife, LaVey. The title, "I Don't Want To Die," is so named, as she whispered these words to me during the night just three days before she went to Heaven. It almost broke my heart because neither one of us could do anything about it. "I love you, Honey."

CAST OF CHARACTERS

MODELS: Using first names, to protect the closeness of the main
CREDITS: Front and back covers by Jim Shrum. (2) a criminal investigator for the DA's office in Santa Rosa, CA, and a retired detective with the Santa Rosa PD Santa Rosa. He is a former President of the Western Regional Negotiator's Association.

MARTHA	Stan's mother
HIRAM	Stan's father
ROYAL	Stan's brother
EWING WALKER	Stan's friend
JOE LOUIS	Himself
GRACIE	Ina's mother
INA	Millie's mother
MILLIE	Main character
TIM	Millie's husband
STAN	Millie's father
INA	Millie's mother
SUPER WONDER	The villain
NELLIE	Millie's friend
HIRAM 2	Lawyer
BEN	Family friend
JACK	Hot shot lawyer
JIM	Millie's son
MARY ANN	Millie's daughter
BRUCE	Millie's Ex
BOB the fisherman	Jim's friend
DR. MARK	Family doctor
DR. KELLY	Main doctor
JUDGE	Wilma Silvera
CLAUDJNE	Jim 2nd wife
SUPER WONDER	As a punk

Most of the characters in this book, since it is a story based on facts, are fictitious names and are not intended to degrade any characters, living or dead, but to give credence to the story line. Some extras have been used.

FOREWORD

This is the true-life story of one brave girl who was raped at about age four while playing jacks with some other girls of the same age. In those days, little girls wore short dresses as the style at time. Neighborhood boys would stand idly by while the girls were playing their various games. Some of the boys were just plain punks, and that is the crux of this story. This story not only touched the lives of the characters in these gaines, but of the lives of people far, far down the line. And that is one of the facts that is completely unnecessary. Did it stop there? No and it never will. Why? Ever hear of "peach tree tea"?

Red Skelton, one of the great comics of all time and a man who is on the square, says it best in his routine about the mean little kid, who muses "if I dood it, I get a whuppin. I dood it."

And he got a Whuppin'. When the author was a kid, he was given a dose of peach tea, right after his brush with authority. His mama would say, "Son go out in the yard and bring me the usual ingredient He didn't need to ask what that was. By now, he knew. He ripped off a slender limb from the peach tree and stripped it of its leaves, etc, and took it to his mama who had him assume the position, whereby she laid it on the seat of learning, and if all went well, he got the point. So, peach tree tea.

But even so it wasn't always effective. In the mid-twenties, you didn't even dare to say the word "rape." Such nasty words were strictly forbidden by the culture administered by the best of the best, so they say. And besides, (so they say) who cares about what happens to little girls, anyway. They'll outgrow it.

Sure they will. Read on, and marbles to doughnuts, you will feel like you've just been dragged through the sewer. Mama would say, "Don't you dare tell anyone, ever, or you won't get a good husband. You probably won't, anyway. This is the story of one little girl who tried to "live with it."

Now, you will find out just what happens to little girls, and one in particular, who tried to "live with it." Go get some Kleenex. You will need it.

If it is any solace to the reader, the author was surprised by the ending, also. Shrum, James D. - Born January 1, 1919 in Gans, Oklahoma. To parents May Bell and Ben Shrum. After moving a few times, due to work changes, they settled in Britton, Oklahoma where young J. D., as he was called in his early years, attended Britton High School and later graduated from Woodland High School in Woodland, CA. Writing for the high school news paper consumed much of his time as "Jim", who also wrote for the town newspaper as sports editor and poet for both papers. As the war in Europe progressed, Jim saw the inequities of a dictator, and wrote two poems concerning this atrocity which were published in the World's Fair Anthology of 1939. As time moved on, he wrote professionally both militarily and in civilian publications. His latest achievements are books,
The Umbrella Theory, Stars in My Crown, Eternal Rape and now *I Don't Want To Die.*

BIOGRAPHY OF THE AUTHOR

Jim is a native of Oklahoma where, as a young teenager, he made friends with Wiley Post and Will Rogers, who would come to town and land in a cow pasture for a runway, and use the barn as a hangar, being very careful walking from their light bi-plane to the safety of civilization. One day a gust of wind (lots of wind in the plains of Oklahoma) blew off Will Rogers flat straw hat (very popular back then) and as it blew through the tumbleweeds and cow patties, Will tried on seven before he found the right one. In his mid-teens Jim came to Woodland, CA and was paroled from high school there. The army got him in 1942, and disqualified him for overseas duty because hiss feet were also flat.

His first assignment was made by Col. David H. Thomas, a top civilian lawyer in Cleveland, who saw his IQ was 157, and had him establish the 484th Sub Depot in Avon Park, Fla. (He couldn't even spell it. But he did it, and was rated superior for his efforts). After the War, it appeared the US was headed for more trouble in the Pacific, so the Navy, under the direct guidance of Admiral Radford, and Two-star holder Fitzhugh Lee, (direct descendant of (Gen. Robert E. Lee) he was directed to establish the ASW and Shipping, Control Offices of the Pacific fleet.

So he did. Why did he stop in Hawaii? A Navy, Chief saw his credentials and asked a silly question? "Would you mind staying, here at Pearl? We need admin men very badly." No question about that. (Well, heck fire. Somebody had to do it). So after the Navy he messed around and got a Law Degree (LL.B.) and an MBA, among others things. Then he taught behavioral science and management for 12 years, and finally, after lecturing on the subjects for a while he wrote a book, *The Umbrella Theory*, and another *Stars in my Crown* and another *I Don't Want to Die*. And for good measure he wrote and published over 200 poems. He is a member of Capital City Lodge and a PM a member of the Scottish Rite and the Ben Mi Shrine. So, there you are.

Part 2

Having written *The Umbrella Theory, Stars in My Crown, Eternal Rape, I Don't Want To Die, I Remember* (a book of poems), and professional writing for over 40 years, the author decided to expand his talents to true stories as much as possible, as they seem to fulfill a vacant spot in his desires to write. A native of Oklahoma, he completed his education in California. He began his working career with the Federal Government before spending eight years in the Army and Navy in the (now it can be told) intelligence department.

Retiring finally in 1981, he did a number of odd assignments, until he became bored with that and turned to his first love, writing. His military superiors often told him with a high IQ, he should take advantage of it. He completely ignored all that as superior flattery. Who knows? With a head full of schooling and lecturing knowledge, he decided to put it on paper, and so he did.

In addition to all that, his investigations led him directly to his typewriter and thence to his computer. And so it goes. Thank you for your kindness in being interested in my work.

Part One

Eternal Rape

CHAPTER 1

We begin this crime against humanity back in the mid-twenties when certain words were considered a sin just because the connotation of the word was a sin. We will use fictitious names throughout to protect the identity of the characters in the story. As the story unfolds, you will see why. The author's law books call the crime, "statutory rape" simply because it occurred against a child under the age of consent. The child was about the age of five. The Good Book defines a child under the age of eight as being faultless and precocious, and directly under the influence and protection of the Almighty, from the House not made with hands, eternal in the Heavens. Thus, this is a crime against the eternal love and protection of One to whom we must someday confess our trespasses.

Millie is the main character in the book, as it is centered around her. She was pushing her fifth birthday. To her, that was a lot of years. And she was happy beyond words. Ina, her mother, was standing in the doorway of their home, watching with pride and joy at the innocence of these little girls, playing jacks, with their little dresses hiked up to be out of the way of the bouncing ball. The punk's name was Bob. And he loved to watch the little girls play, as he got a big charge out of looking at their legs, even as small as they were. Even though far younger than he, he had other ideas, always had. So he continued with their games. Hide and go seek, drop the handkerchief, etc., To Bob the Punk, spin the bottle was his favorite game.

INA

    This was a balmy day in May when all the kids were home from school, and just itching to get into their favorite games. Bob the Punk, loved to watch them play jacks, so he could watch their little turns and jumps to get out of the way of the bouncing ball. So he positioned himself right across from Millie, as she was the cutest of the girls, and he really wanted to get his hands on her. Of course Millie was cute. Her mother, Ina, was voted the most beautiful woman in Payson, Utah. But she only had eyes for Stan, that handsome hunk who had to drop out of school to help save the family farm. Stan was so bashful about his courting. Stan was anything but dumb. He only looked at her out of the corner of his eyes, so she wouldn't notice, but she did, anyway. On graduation day from high school, Stan was clever enough to position himself just across the isle from her at the ceremony so that when they were called up to the podium to receive their diplomas, there was good old Stan right by her side.

    Of course, that was some time ago, and Millie had become prettier and Stan had become more handsome by the day and more rugged from the work on his father's farm. Then, along came little Millie to brighten up their lives, like nothing else ever could.

These beautiful ceremonies. All happening after they had gone through the temple, just added more glory to a wonderful pair. No happier couple existed. They were completely unaware of the evil intentions of Bob, the Punk. H seemed friendly toward the kids, and they seemed to accept him. Now, since Bob, the Punk, had taken in those around him, he was more aggressive. And Millie? Cute as a button, brown wavy hair, creamy complexion, red ruby lips, and a smile that would charm anyone. And, when she laughed, It almost seemed like an angel whispering to God. Nothing escaped Bob, the Punk. Nothing.

![SUPER WONDER THE PUNK]

As the game of jacks progressed, Bob, the Punk, kept his eyes glued in the well developed legs of Millie. When the game lost momentum, Bob quickly suggested to Millie that they go to his house for some cookies and milk. Little girls of five, are so innocent and gullible, they believe almost anything a "friend" suggests. So into his house they went. Since his mother and dad were both at work, he had the house to himself. Millie became nervous, and asked, "Bob, where are the cookies and milk?" "In due time." He said. "First, I want to show you something." And he did. This frightened Millie, and she began to cry. "Shut up, and you won't get hurt. But if you keep this up, I'm going to hurt you."

"First, let's play this game I know." And he proceeded to rape her, and mangled her body's organs so badly it was doubtful if she could ever conceive, or even to consume a marriage vow. Blood was all over, but Millie was so petrified by now she couldn't even cry. He then had her close her eyes, while he hummed the church hymn, "I Need Thee Every Hour" which seemed to soothe her. "This is all part of the game," he continued, and proceeded to the act all over again.

By now, Millie was in such intense pain, she could barely remain conscious. And Bob continued his actions until he fell on top of Millie, exhausted. Bob said, "Now, don't cry. Millie. It's all part of the game." Millie just lay there, unable to move. And now, she began to cry in earnest. Big, deep, sobs, as though her very soul and heart were breaking. As her sobs began to subside, she noticed Bob had left the room, so she took advantage of this respite, and left by the back door and ran home as fast as she could, and curled up in her own bed and cried herself to sleep.

As Ina came through the front door, she sensed something was wrong, and called out to Millie. "In here, Mama." Ina was in a state of panic at the sight she beheld of her pride and joy, Mille. She has never run into anything like this before, and she was near to passing out herself. She had heard of this happening to other people, but this was different. Should I tell Stan? What should I do? So, she did just what was the custom in those days. "Now, Millie, I know you have been through a lot of pain, and it still hurts. But everyone says never to tell anyone else, or people will blame you, and you will never get a good husband. So, will you promise me you will be silent about this the rest of your life?" Among her sobs, Millie said, "Yes, Mama. I promise."

Should I tell Stan? Heavens, no. He is my husband, and I love him dearly, but he is a big blabbermouth. I'll just have to keep this bottled up inside. If this gets out, Millie will be scarred for life. No. It has to be a secret. We'll move. That's what we'll do. Go to Long Beach, California, that's what. We have relatives, there. A completely bewildered Stan had no idea what was going on, but the light of his life wanted to move, so that's just what we'll do. And they moved to Long Beach where Uncle Roe had a big business, so he took good acre of the Sargent Family.

Poor Millie. What man would have a spoiled woman? Millie was doomed to be single for the rest of her life. No husband, no kids. No future. What to do? Nothing was ever what it should be. The mailman was leaning on the doorbell while she was daydreaming about Uncle Roe helping them. "Hope it's good news, ma'am", he said. No such luck. "I Want You" it said to Stan. What a welcome that was going to be for Stan when he came home from work on his father's farm.

As Stan ripped open the telegram, he had a sinking feeling it was not going to be good news. It wasn't. "I want you" it said. Sure. Stan worked on his father's farm, and he was badly needed there. But Stan? He was all man. He said, simply, "Ina, my country needs me. I have to go. But don't worry. God is mightier than the sword. I'll be back. "Then he took a good look at Ina's face. Something was wrong. And it wasn't the war draft.

This notice says to report to the train station Monday morning at eight o'clock. I can do that. It's not like going to the fields at 8 o'clock. That hit Stan like a ton of bricks. "Oh, good gosh. I won't be here anymore. What are we gonna do, Ina? You can't work in the fields like I do. And we ain't got any money to hire it done. Just then a knock rattled the front door. It was the Bishop. "Stan, news travels fast. I hear you are drafted?" "Yes, I am, and we're trying to figure out how we re gonna get this done, or lose the farm, even if it is my Dad's." "Well, that's what I came here about. We have a lot of men who are retired, and just raring to do something. They don't want no pay, just something to do. They have retirement pay to hold them over, so they're OK. All right by you?"

"Sure, it is. I was worried about losing the farm. Now I won't worry no more about my wife and kid. They can stay with my folks. And Ina couldn't get the words out fast enough. "Now, Bishop, don't you fret about us. We'll be all right. And I'll take good care of Millie. The Bishop got the inference. But how in blue blazes did he find out about Millie? So the Bishop let the matter drop. "Yes, ma'am. They have retirement pay to hold them over, so they're OK. All right by you?"

"Sure, it is. I was worried about losing the farm. Now I won't worry no more about my wife and kid. They can stay with my folks. And Ina couldn't get the words out fast enough. "Now, Bishop, don't you fret about us. We'll be all right. And I'll take good care of Millie. The Bishop got the inference. But how in blue blazes did he find out about Millie? "Yes, ma'am. You know best." And off he went. Since this was Friday, there was a lot of fast moving to do. Stan had to get packed and ready to be a private. Mille said, "Now, Stan. You know what they say about them French girls. Don't you be lookin' their way, or they'll be after you. I think you're mighty handsome, you know. And so will they." This really hit home. He had never really thought of himself as being attractive to other women, so he said, "Now, don't you worry about that. I just got eyes for you, and you know that. You bein' the prettiest girl in town, and bein' married to me. Ain't that enough?" "I hope so. You look at my picture, once in a while. You hear?" And the alarm clock did its thing early Monday morning, and now, it's cryin' time. "Love you with all my heart, honey." "Love you, too." And Stan went to war.

CHAPTER 2

"Son. Wake up" Shouted his mother. And Stan slowly opened his eyes and looked at his mother with a dazed expression. With a slow smile of indulgence, Martha twiddled Stan's nose and repeated, "It's time to rise and shine. The Army bus will be here at ten. You don't want to miss it." "Oh, no, I surely wouldn't" with a little dry humor. Stan had worked all his life on his father's farm after school. together with his brother, Hiram, and he was in great physical condition. He didn't need the Army doctor to tell him that. But he did. "What a dream," he started with his mother. She listened intensively, as she always did when one of her offspring wanted to talk. This mother knew how to be a mother instinctively. And what did she get in return? An undying love, no less. "Mom, I don't know if I ought to tell you this dream or not, it isn't very nice." "Now, son, when have I ever refused to listen to something you feel is important, or unseemly?"

"You're right, Mom. I dreamed I came home from the Army and asked Millie to marry me, and she did." "Well, now, son, I don't see much wrong with that. You know how I feel about Millie, like she was one of my own. Not only was she voted the prettiest girl in Payson, but I think she is the smartest. She'll make some nice young man a wonderful wife, and I hope it's you." "Yeah, Mom, I hope so, too." Stan fidgeted some before going on with his dream, "I dreamed we had a little girl with light brown hair, big brown eyes, a dimple in each cheek, a personality that would melt anyone, and a tinkling laugh that I felt sounded like an angel whispering to God." "Wow. What a dream. When will you finish that dream?" "I don't know, Mom. But it's what I've been day dreaming for right along," mused Stan. The Army courier just had to pick this time to deliver Stan his khakis, even though spring was still a little on the chilly side. Martha stepped out of the room while Stan hurriedly slipped into his wardrobe for the next session of life, for whatever length of time that would be.

Hesitantly, he opened the bedroom door and shyly walked up to his mother as she looked out the window into space, and turned around with an audible gasp, and her eyes misted over as she looked at her handsome son for the first time in an Army uniform. "Oh, my. Aren't you the one," she whispered, afraid to say too much. Afraid she might cry, or do something else that might cause Stan to regret his leaving her at this point in her life. But Martha was not the maudlin type. She was made of strong stock, and carried herself like a winner, always. The only thing she could do under the circumstances was to grab her son, and hug him with all her might for the last time before watching him march off with the Rainbow Division, the most feared division in the United States Army. As Stan closed the door for the last time, Martha let go, and the tears flowed freely, as they would with any mother watching her son proudly march off into his unknown fate, with God's blessing.

Stan looked to his right and shook hands with a ruggedly handsome man with eyes steady and muscles bulging from hard labor in the fields on his farm. "My name's Walker. Ewing Walker. People call me 'Eu' for short." "My name's Stan Sargent. Not my rank, just my name." And both men had a good laugh. "ATTENTION. FORWARD, MARCH," shouted the First Sergeant. And everyone in the block applauded and yelled last good wishes at the men as they marched off into their destiny. By the time the Division reached the busses that would take them to the troop ship headed for the boot of Italy, and for some, their dirty, rotten, stinking place where they would be laid to rest, sore feet prevailed, and backs ready for someone to try to get the kinks out of the sore muscles.

True to the conduct of war, they were met at the dock with guns blazing and mortar falling indiscriminately among the new recruits, making instant widows and orphans right and left. Stan noticed Eu standing upright and firing his M1 at chosen targets with the calm of a real soldier. A fine example of bravery for Stan to emulate. And he did. No time for daydreaming here. Just you or them. Stan had never been a coward, and now was the ideal time for his backbone to show. All of a sudden, his thoughts returned to Millie. What was she doing now? And his mother, and father, and brother, and the friends at church? Would they be proud of him in his finest hour? He was always respected and liked. Never one to shirk his duty, no matter what. As Stan and Eu, side by side, fought gallantly for their country, they never gave a quarter nor asked for a quarter. Real men, and it showed by the smiles of gratitude from the old timers in the Fightingest Division of the US Army, the Rainbow Division, proud to the core.

When the winds of war shifted, the men literally dropped to the ground where they stood, or walked a few yards to a grassy knoll and took a well deserved rest. Ewing looked over at Stan, "Hey, don't tell me you're not a professional soldier. You're the fightingest man I ever saw. A real warrior." "No," said Stan. "I just didn't want to make friends with a chunk of lead." And this made Eu laugh till he had to stop and take his breath. Capt Joe Louis came over, stood in front of Stan, and said, "Man, I'm glad you're not my enemy. My congratulations. My colonel just put you and Walker in for the Silver Star. You saved a lot of lives. Both ours and theirs." With a big thumbs up, he went for a cold drink of water from the stream nearby. Eu and Stan exchanged grins, and lay back for a few minutes of well deserved rest.

"For some unexplained reason, I had the most fearsome feeling, as though Stan were in some sort of trouble," Ina said to her mother, as they listened to the evening news. "No," said Gracie, "Stan is all man. He can take care of himself." A knock at the door brought them to attention in a hurry. The telegram was from a Capt. Joe Louis. "Regret to inform you, ma, Stan was ambushed from a church door. Very cowardly of the Axis. His helmet was creased on one side by an Ml and hit on the other side by a 50 Caliber which pierced his helmet and his head and came out the rear of his helmet. He lay face down in the mud and slush until we could get to him. Ewing was hit in the left shoulder with mortar, very severely, trying to rescue Stan. He finally dragged Stan to safety but at a terrible price of his own. We lose two more wonderful medals here and proud to do so. Though I may be a little darker than these two men, I would gladly give my life for them. (Signed) Joe Louis.

CHAPTER 3

And Stan goes back home to break the good news to Ina. She still looked worried but the strength of the woman was amazing. What to do? We can't stay here with that punk on the loose. He would certainly try this again or at least to some other innocent girl. Without saying why, she alerted the other mothers in the neighborhood about the punk. Some had already had brushes with him, so they took it seriously. They say, there is a bully in every group of people or organization, and Ina believed this now. It certainly seemed to be true, but in Payson? It seemed improbable, but it was true. This is a quiet little town, with love flowing from every door. Now this is spoiled. For the most part, the people here are the genteel type. So why does there have to be a bully here? But the Chief of Police knows. Bob the punk was given a parole by a friend of the Chiefs, who just happens to be his uncle, and is no angel, himself. He was elected Chief of Police by the populace, so there can be no crying about it. More than one lady had complained about the freshness of the chief, but to no avail. He was after the pretty ones mainly, but he had the common sense to stay away from Ina as Stan was the runner-up in the state heavyweight division. No, Sir, he wanted his ugly face to stay ugly.

Ina was voted the prettiest girl in BYU, so naturally the punk would like to make time with her. Never happen, and he knew it. She only had eyes for Stan, and he for her. What a pair they made, Ina's mother, Gracie, needed a few groceries for the week end, and as she was riddled with arthritis, Ina volunteered to go for her. As ha passed the chiefs car, he made some very inflammatory remarks, but kept his eyes straight ahead so he could say he had not been talking to Ina. No matter. It still made

Ina see red, and she proceeded to tell off the chief in the choicest of words she could muster, and the chiefs face turned beet red.

He couldn't stand it any longer. So he foolishly jumped out of his patrol car and threw Ina in the back seat of the car unmercifully. "I'll teach you to respect the arm of the law, he shouted. His outburst got the attention of the people nearby, and one man, who was wearing his collar backward, asked the chief, "What has she done, Chief?" "She talked disrespectfully to me, that's what she done." "Well, sir, just what was it she said," persisted the Priest. "I don't remember, but I don't like it, anyway." "Chief, my brother is a lawyer, and I'll have him draw up a complaint against this lady, but first, I have to know what she said." Now, the chief was completely rattled, and said, "aw, forget it. Now get out of my car, woman, you're stinking it up'" As Ina composed herself, she thanked the priest for his kindness, and saw just the flickering of a smile cross his face, which caused ha to burst out laughing. How little we know of life.

Aid comes in the most unusual packages. Various people have been given missions to fulfill while others are still searching for theirs. This Catholic Priest was a good friend of the family. And it was he, who won the heavyweight championship from Stan. Made them both respect and love one another without a word being said. How wonderful is our democracy. And so many times we take it for granted. Where do we get all this? The Good Book says the strength of the Almighty is awesome, and not to be taken lightly, ha had taken several courses on the deity at BYU, so she knew she was in good hands. And then it hit her. Oh, my gosh, what will I do if Stan finds out about this? She knew what Stan would do, chief or no chief Somebody was going to get their block knocked off. Oh, well. On to get Gracie's groceries. When she got home, Stan met her at the door with his well known reception, a big hug and a kiss. Ina looked at his eyes to see if she could read anything there, but he was a master at hiding his thoughts. This always got to Ina, so she grabbed him and said, "Don't you have anything to tell me?" "Well, yes, I do. Somebody gave the chief a big, swollen black eye."

CHAPTER 4

As time passed, everything seemed to settle down to peace and quiet. The rough shod neighbors, husband and wife, had split up as the husband couldn't keep his hands to himself, and in the process, got thrown in jail on charges of sexual abuse by his other neighbor, plus a busted nose thrown in for good measure. All this on the part of the lady's husband, who was visiting in the neighborhood. The sheriff kept out of the fracas as he was just as bad. After 24 hours had passed, the sheriff released his unruly prisoner on the grounds of good behavior, such as it is. As Mighty passed in front of Ina's house, (he liked to be called Mighty) she tried to be friendly and keep good relations with the neighborhood trash, but it just didn't work. "Keep your snotty thoughts to yourself, woman. I don't need your sympathy." That cut Ina to the bone, as she was.

Mighty didn't miss his estranged wife at all, as he had a following of the same kind to his liking, and they reveled at his attention. This was not missed at all by his no-good son, Bob, who yearned to be just like his father, if he was indeed his father. Mighty never gave it a thought to see that his son had the necessities of life, and most of the time he left Bob alone to root for himself And this was the day Bob picked to show his "old man", as he called his father, that he could do anything Mighty did, and maybe even better. He knew that every day about one hour from now, the small girls in the area would gather on the sidewalk in front of Ina's house for jacks, spin the bottle, or any game they had. So now, he made his plans. He had been daydreaming about this plan ever since the Sargents had come back to Payson. They thought they were so high and mighty, he would certainly show them who was high and mighty.

He leisurely took his time about his arrival on the scene, and the little girls, all about five and six, had already gathered for their daily game and were having the time of their lives, laughing and playing as they always did. Bob began to lick his lips in anticipation of accomplishing his horrid deed. He had a sack of candy, almost all gone by now, but he made a big show of his love for the remaining candy in the sack, even to the point of smacking his lips and grinning like a hyena about to discover the difference between little boy hyenas and little girl hyenas. Little Millie, sharp as a tack, noticed this, and immediately became interested in candy, as any little five year old would do. Nelly, Millie's good friend, noticed all this byplay, and thought this nice young man might have enough candy for all of them. Bob made it clear that was not the case, but took advantage of this ideal opening to say, "Tell you what I'll do. Have Millie follow me to my home where my mother has just made the best fudge you ever tasted, and I'll give her enough fudge for all of you to have two pieces apiece. What do you say?" Oh, my. Nothing this great has ever happened before, so the girls immediately begged Millie to go this fine person to get them all some of the lip smacking candy.

And now, Bob was in his glory, as he was just about to have his way with that little ball of beauty and desire that he had dreamed about for two years now, but no opening had ever been laid in his lap before. And now it had. Even all the little girls were on his side, now. He couldn't miss. Just think. A fifteen year old dream (he imagined himself as a dream boat) how could he miss? So little Millie, ever the one to do whatever an adult said, as she was taught in Sunday School, was about to receive her heart's dream of some mighty fine fudge, and even some for her friends. This was indeed a beautiful day, and all the little girls were anxiously awaiting Millie's return. Bur it didn't happen. They waited a long time, and eventually, had to go home, not knowing why Millie didn't return.

Just inside Bob's home, Millie asked where was the fudge? And Bob, ever the deceitful and evil person that he was, took Millie's hand and led her to the couch on the back porch, where he gave Millie a small piece of fudge to satisfy her appetite. Then he told Millie there was a big spider that had crawled just under Millie's dress and he would find it and kill it so it wouldn't bite Millie. Millie was all for this. She was afraid of spiders, anyway, Then Bob did the strangest thing. He unzipped his pants, and began to do something Millie had never seen before. Bob noticed this, and told Millie she must help him so he could get that bad spider.

She gladly agreed. And she agreed to do what Bob said, so the spider could be caught, and it wouldn't bit her. Bob said, "We can't ask my mother to help as she got picked up by the sheriff for being drunk." And this was when Millie felt the strange sensation of horrible pain, and she began to cry. Bob told her, "If you cry, that spider will hear you and come running after you." And this very great pain continued for the longest time, and Millie could no longer contain her cries, as this pain kept getting greater and greater, and Bob seemed to enjoy making her cry, as he smiled and began greater movements than before. It seemed like forever, and now Millie felt hot sensations as though someone was pouring hot water on her body, which actually was blood coming from little Millie's own body.

And then it stopped. And Bob gave a deep sigh, which puzzled Millie. But the pain still continued to wrack Millie's body. For some reason unknown to Millie, Bob took her to the door and said, "Get lost." Millie wasn't lost. She knew where she was, but the pain was so great she didn't know what to do except run home and see if her mother could make the pain go away. She opened the front door and ran crying to her mother in the kitchen, and leaving a long trail of blood trailing behind her. Ina took one look and almost fainted at the sight. She grabbed her Millie and ran to the bathroom as fast as she could, and started warm water in the bathtub as fast as she could, all the while undressing Millie and puffing her in the warm water and cleansing the blood off of her, and asking Millie a dozen questions all at the same time. As the story unfolded, ma then knew what had happened, and her compassion for little Millie knew no boundaries. Both crying, and Ina knew instinctively what to do, and applied some of her own medications to the injured area, and in her own mind, thought of taking Stan's Army .38 and making a bee line to Bob's house, and finishing the story. But then, common sense told her she could not take another person's life, as it said in one of the Ten Commandments. Her mind was filled with questions. What must she do? Call Stan in from the Fields? Call the sheriff? Does she tell anyone? Who would believe such a story from a five year old?

The best she could do was comfort Millie, give her some pain medicine, and wait for Stan to come in from his meager work in the fields. He could do very little work, and the easiest at best, and then go home and wait, if only a little bit, for the pain to subside. As Stan walked through the door, he knew something was wrong. "Ha, I can tell that something is very wrong. What is it?" "Now, Stan, before I tell you, promise me you will do absolutely nothing until we talk this over." "All right, Ina, I promise." "Stan, from what Millie has told me, and from my own observation of her little body, Bob has done a terrible thing to her. She seems to be alright, but she has lost a lot of blood. I don't know what the inside of her body is like, but she screams a lot and is in terrible pain." Stan was crying visibly now, and started to get up from his chair. "Now, Stan, you promised." "I know, but this has really done something to me that has never happened before." "I understand, Stan. But we have to look into the future." This, from the stronger emotionally of the two.

"If this gets out, do you know what people will say? It was her fault. I know. How can a little five year old cause this to happen? But they will blame her anyway. I know exactly how you feel. And so do I. Lets see if we know anyone we can trust with this horrible crime. Yes. It is a crime. Our cousin, Ben, the lawyer, says this is called Statutory. But he also called it something else. He calls it a living death. And I wouldn't be surprised if turns out to be just that, a living death. At best it's statutory. I can't bring myself to say that word that goes with it, but you know what it is." Stan had reduced his crying, as had Ina, but the mist was heavy in their eyes. "I think we ought to call Ben, and see what he says," offered Ina, ever the level headed in tight situations such as this. The next morning, Ben rushed over to their home as fast as he could. This had come as an awful shock to him, as he was the God Father to Millie and couldn't bring himself to believe this really happened. Of course he knew Bob, and knew what he was capable of, as well as Bob's own father. His feelings were like most others. This never happens to your family, it happens to other families.

Ben was fidgeting like no other situation he had experienced. Little Millie. The apple of his eye. His head was loaded with information from his law books. Yes. He knew exactly what the action was called. And, yes, he did refer to the action as a living death, because it is in the persons own psyche, and never leaves, nor cam it be expunged by hypnotism, nor any other method known to man. It can have a chilling effect on the person now or somewhere in the future, by causing some form of dementia. As Ben was fond of saying, God Said it, I believe it, and that's that. How will little Millie react from this episode in her young life? Will she outlive it.? Some do. Some don't. Those that don't or can't outlive it, go through what I call a living death, as they are still alive, but living a horrifying existence, and in most cases, creating a living death to those who must care for them until they are called home to be with the Almighty. And looking at Millie right now as she has dropped off to sleep from this terrible experience, Yes, I too feel deeply moved, and without prior schooling in law, my first impulse would be to break that (blank) neck. Oh, would I love to do that. They say a little knowledge is a dangerous thing, or words to that effect. And that is because a LITTLE knowledge does not give you the lull picture, and you would then probably commit some crime yourself.

"And that would cause my aunt Minnie to say, OH, FUDGE. Meaning, of course, Oh, shucks, I made a booboo." And then, the adults got down to business of frying to find some solution to the problem of little Millie, and still do her justice. Should we keep still about it? Should we confront Bob about it? Should we tell "Jailbird" Mighty about what his son has done? Should we string up Bob to the nearest Oak tree, and cut off everything that hangs down? Should we go to the authorities about it? (It's almost a given they will laugh about it, they have in the past), Maybe we better give this some more thought. Millie seems to feel that if Millie carries this openly though adulthood, that she won't find a suitable husband, and this caught the fancy of most of the committee, and there it stands. Life from age five to 19 or 20, and looking for a husband? What a load to carry. Anyway, the motion carried And good luck, Millie. May God Bless.

MILLIE, INA & STAN

CHAPTER 5

Poor Millie. What a life she's had so far. Only five and she has experienced adult problems. As the neighborhood kids (each lived about a quarter of a mile apart) began to gather for their after noon games, they were the chatterboxes as usual. Even Millie didn't seem the worse for wear. But since Ina and the others didn't wish to involve a doctor to examine Millie for even nothing more than some sort of disease, let alone some sort of tearing of the internal tissues so vital to a woman's good health now and later in life. However, it being in the mid to upper 20's, doctors were seldom called or examined for this sort of thing. The little tyke seems to be holding up extremely well considering her recent experience. And, wouldn't you know, the mailman appeared seemingly on cue. "Can I have the mail?" timidly asked Millie. "Of course you can, Millie. You live here." And he was indeed a prince of a fellow.

As the other kids dispersed to their separate homes, Millie took her prizes into the house for her mother to look at. As Ina opened the first letter, she noticed some blood on Millie's left leg. "Honey, did you hurt your leg? I see some blood on your left leg." "No, Mama, I never hurt myself that boy, Bob, hurt me." Then it hit Ina like a bombshell. This brave little angel is still bleeding from yesterday. Her eyes misted over in spite of herself. Something is going to have to be done, she thought. Don't know what, but after I clean up my little Millie, I'm going to do some heavy thinking. Stan is going to be mad as a wet hornet, but I've got to have a plan in mind to offset his anger. Millie was so good to take medicine and to be patched up when she skinned her knees. After the brief sponge bath, Ina made sure Millie was all right. Stan came home from the fields at about 6:30, tired from the easy work he had done for the day, but he was under orders from the army doctors to take life easy, or he would hear from them. Say what you want to about army or navy doctors, but most of them are very concerned about the health of the military personnel.

As usual, Stan made a big deal out of reunions with his beautiful wife, and she loved every minute of it. This was her man, and she was so proud of him. Why? He never complained about his back, but she knew he was in pain most of the time, and the brace had to be worn as tightly as he could stand it or he would not even be able to stand up. Wars were awful. They should be outlawed. But who could do that? They were fought between nations, and promulgated by the men of power, who wanted more power even yet. God knows about this. Why doesn't he do something about it? She knew the answer to this, but, of course, she didn't like that answer either. At their ladies club last month, one lady, a very good philosopher, said she thought those big shots went to war because they couldn't disagree without being disagreeable. Well, made sense, of sorts. Time to talk to Stan before he found out about it first. "Stan, have you ever thought about moving away from here? I mean, we've been here quite a while, and your dad has never asked even for a nickel, and quite rightly, we do owe him." "Yeah, Ina, I know, and I feel bad about that, but I just didn't know what to do about it."

"Stan, do you think Uncle Roe might have something in Long Beach? He owns a big manufacturing plant there, and he might be able to help us out." "All right. I'll write him a letter and see what he says. But I don't want charity, Ina. I want to earn my way, back or no back." And the letter went off in the morning mail. When Roe saw the letter, opened by his secretary, he sat at his desk and gave it some serious thought. Roe was one of the most dedicated men in the church, and he never turned his back on anyone who needed assistance from anything or for any reason. He liked Stan, and knew of his record in the Rainbow Division, so he never hesitated to write Stan a letter telling him he had an opening and he needed to fill it as soon as Stan could get there. He owned an apartment building, and saved an apartment for the Sargents as soon as they arrived. They were so happy, and Roe was even happier to be able to do something for one of his own in need. The second day they were in Long

Beach, Millie had some bleeding that Roe noticed. Never one to turn his back on one in need, he called his friend, Dr. Sehr, who came right over to Roe's home, and, with Stan and Ina's permission, took care of Millie's problem. And it never occurred again.

One week into their stay in Long Beach, Ina soon learned that she was allergic to the oil fields nearby, and hesitated to tell Uncle Roe, but he noticed it anyway. He said, "ma, I didn't know about your allergy to oil, and neither did you. The only relief you will get at this day and age is to live away from oil fields. I hate to tell you this, and if you will let me, I'll pay for your move wherever it might be." "What a great man," was Ina's first thought. She talked it over with Stan, and the next day, they decided to try Sacramento. It was touted to be smog and allergy free, so maybe it would be the place. That was Brigham Young's first thought when he looked out of the wagon parked on the high ledge overlooking Salt Lake Valley. And he was right, too. As the newcomers came within sight of the Sacramento Valley, Stan said, "Uncle Roe was right, too. This is the place." And as they settled in an inexpensive apartment, Stan said to a startled Ina, "Honey, I just don't know what I'm gonna do. I've tried to not show it, but I just can't stand to have this brace as tight as it is. And if I take it off, I'm gonna be in trouble. Can you see if there is a doctor in any of the south Wards? Maybe they will know what I can do?"

CHAPTER 6

What to do. What to do. Tim, who had nearly always been the strong one, to whom others flowed for some sort of assistance, was, now, searching for answers. He had never encountered Alzheimer's disease, nor any person or information relative to the subject. Could it have had it's roots in their 1950 life in Hawaii? Who knows? Hawaii was the lifelong dream of so many people, how could it be anything but great? Balmy weather, soft breeze, temperature for the most part in the highly desirable range, everyone dressed about as casual as you can imagine without taking any more clothing off, no one is in a hurry to get to any destination, almost anything goes, and sometimes does, tide gently kissing the shore, birds of all species singing their tunes for all to enjoy, and they do, no, it just doesn't seem possible that anything bad could come from paradise, as it is many times called, and rightfully so.

Tim had been given permission from Capt. Fitzhugh Lee, and CDR Wayne Snider, to send for his wife and six year old son, to join him for his official duty in Oahu, on the Hill, as it is called. It is a four story building, (above ground) where Admiral Radford and his huge staff of high powered (lots of high rank) men and women needed to operate the Pacific Fleet during the Korean conflict, (not a war, don't you know, just a military police action). As Tim met them disembarking from the troop ship, little Jim 2nd gave his Daddy a stuffed animal he had saved for the occasion, and that made it "official" Happy? Not the word, but it will do. The six year old was spotless, as his Mama, Millie, always kept him. And now, all seemed right with the world, so how could anything negative happen? Tim had already asked the nice people running Fort DeRussy, for a limited stay there with his newly arrived family, and it was immediately approved. That the way it was in Paradise. No muss, no hiss, just happy people.

For over a month, no vacancies, anywhere. While at church the following Sunday, Tim introduced his wife and son to George Q. Cannon, 3rd, who immediately asked if they had found a suitable place to stay, but, alas, not so. What did the one and only Bro. Cannon do? "I just happen to have a few apartments in my name here, and you can have one of them until you can find suitable naval housing. Sound OK?" "Wow. Thank you so much," shot out of Millie. Problem solved. After about two weeks, Tim found a naval Quonset hut empty so another problem was solved. And where was this hut? About 100 yards from the shores of the beautiful blue Pacific Ocean where Millie and Little Jimmy just had to visit practically every day (summer time from school, you see) until they were both as brown as any native alive. Tim had been given the task of establishing the ASW and Shipping Control Offices for the Pacific Fleet, so he did.

Sometimes, Tim would have enough time to go home to his hut for lunch, and perhaps a little smooching with Millie, and then return to his excellent position on the Hill. One fine day, as he was approaching the off ramp to the Hill from the highway, a naval car was stopped at the stop sign, awaiting its turn to enter the highway. (No such thing as Freeways at the time, you see). Riding in the back seat of the sedan was a commander who was stationed at the hill in a high position. As Tim turned in front of the sedan, the CDR started making a few notes of Tim's action. Rank has its privileges you know, oh yes it does. Except, if it rubs someone the wrong way. The CDR who had been "wronged" by an enlisted man, namely, Tim, who turned in front of his car while he was riding in it, immediately had Tim stand in front of him while the CDR proceeded to chew, chew, chew until he ran out of breath. "That's all. Go back to work, and don't you ever run afoul of me again, you hear?" "Yes, sir."

As Tim returned to his desk, Capt. Lee routinely asked Tim why he was so late returning to work, not that he gave a tiddly whoop. So, Tim was under obligation to explain why, as he valued his friendship with the

Captain so greatly. "Now, just a minute. Did you just tell me you had the right-of way since you were turning into the Hill road from the highway, and giving the proper signal in doing so?" "Yes, sir. That is what happened, and I caught holy heck for it, so I apologized to the commander for violating his rank." The captain seldom shows emotion. He doesn't have to. But his face began to turn beet red, and Tim thought he was really in for it.

The captain picked up his phone, and very sweetly asked the commander if he could come to his office if it wasn't too much trouble. Now, the commander knew for a fact that Tim was in for the (blank) eating out of all time, so he came sailing through the door with a big smile on his face and shoved Tim to one side while he had the whole view of the Captain. Don't some of these enlisted men ever learn? Officers are truly the backbone of the Navy, and it was way past time they learned that, the hard way, was preferable. "Yes, sir, Captain, I presume you have had a little chat with this so-called navy man?"

"Well, as a matter of fact, I have. "Would be nice enough to tell me your side of the problem?" "I would be delighted to, Sir." And he did. When he finished, he gave a sarcastic grin to Tim and a condescending smile to the Captain. And he shouldn't have done that. Anyone that knew the captain would tell you, don't do that. The captain, face getting redder by the minute, explained that Tim had the right-of-way, and asked if the good commander had ever served on one of the rust-buckets patrolling the Formosa Straits, to which the commander nonchalantly said, "no." The captain gave the commander a look that would have fried a steak well-done, and asked, "Commander, have you ever been informed to say "sir" when addressing a higher rank?" "Oh, yes, sir, I apologize, sir." It was then the captain proceeded to explain the rules of the road and the rules of the Navy on those roads, in such a manner, that the commander looked pleadingly at Tim for help, but never got. He could now envision himself aboard one of those "rust buckets" (actually the worst destroyers in the navy) and knew beyond a doubt he was headed for one. My, oh my, rank does have its privileges. "Dismissed, Commander." And after the door had closed, the Captain gave Tim a knowing look and smiled as he said, "I'm proud to be on the square, aren't you, Tim?"

CHAPTER 7

As Tim went back to his desk, he contemplated the events of the day, and said to himself, there just seems to be problems wherever you are, so make the best of it, and smile. So he smiled. Captain Lee had been watching Tim to see how he was taking the turn of events, and when he saw Tim smile, he knew he had made the right choice in selecting the head of the administrative force. And further thinking by the captain, would Tim make a good officer, and if so, what rank? He decided Tim would make full lieutenant easily. So, what did he do? He pulled Tim's record out of his desk, selected the necessary information from it, and yelled, "Tim. Get in here". He did it on purpose, and Tim came hastily into the captain's office, stood at attention, and barked, "Yeoman First reported as ordered, sir." "Knock it off, Tim, you knew I was just teasing you." "Yes sir, I knew, and when I get to be Master of my Lodge, you better mind your manners, when you address me." And they both had a good laugh out of it. There is no better camaraderie than that of respect between officer and enlisted man when they are both cut from t he same cloth, and that what exists here between Capt. Lee and Tim. And they both knew it

Tim reflected on all this, and his off duty life with his beautiful wife and handsome son. What more could a man ask? Life was gloriously wonderful, and he had to smile again. What did Tim intend to do when the work was all done this afternoon? Why, go to the beach and play in the surf with his wife and son, as they so often do. Paradise? It did seem so. One sour note crept into Tim's daydreams. "You. Take these rolls of movies of mine and mail them. Do you hear me?" "Yes, sir" All this from a commander who felt that enlisted men were his personal flunkies. Was this within hearing distance of Capt. Lee.? Indeed it was. Without throwing cold water on an officer's ego, Capt Lee waited until the next day and asked Tim if indeed he had mailed the commander's movies? "Well, sir," answered Tim "When I got to a mailbox I looked in my jacket pocket to mail the movies, and they must have somehow fallen out without me knowing it. I'll go back tomorrow and see if I can find them." "You're a good man, Tim. I'm glad we're friends." And the Captain went back in his office and closed the door? Why did he do that? And Tim heard the captain laughing his head off. Then I knew.

And Tim had to smile at his memory of these past activities. Sometimes, life was worth while. But, the telephone in his bedroom jolted him out of his reverie. It was one of the Hospice nurses calling to see how Millie was. That ended Tim's reverie for the moment, but it did provide a slight diversion from time to time to relieve him of the pressures of realism. Tim was so grateful to the Hospice program for their help. He would be in a pretty bad shape without their splendid help, both mental and help in caring for the most wonderful woman in the world. Just then, Millie let loose with a string of cuss words that almost curled Tim's hair. The Hospice lady heard all this and hastily yelled for Tim to pick up the phone again. "Tim, I heard all of that, and I'm glad I did. Don't be alarmed by any of that. When people are smitten by Alzheimer's, they are no longer themselves, but are at the mercy of a vicious and overpowering brain disorder. Do you understand?" "No, I don't," replied Tim. "Millie is one of the most religious persons I have ever known, and that is what I like about her." "Tim, get used to almost anything said or done by Millie. It really won't be her doing it."

When Millie finally stopped her tirade, Tim asked her where she had heard all these words. There were some even new to Tim. Millie replied, "I heard them from the girls in High School. That's where, and because you were the bastard that tore up my insides after you raped me, that's why I don't let you get near me for the past years, and I don't know how many and I don't care. NO, DON'T TOUCH ME. You son-of-a-bitch, Get away from me. I don't want to sleep in the same bed with you, but I have to. I can't do anything about that." And yet, that same night, Millie whispered in Tim's ear, "I love you. Tim. And I always will. I want you to be my husband when we go to Heaven." Tim didn't know if she beard his reply or not, but he said it anyway, "Honey, we were married in the Temple for all time and Eternity. And I still mean it. I love you more than life itself, and I can't help it. Yes, I want to be your husband when we go to Heaven."

Yes, Tim remembers all these things happening as though it were yesterday. And what would he have done without the help of the Hospice program? He shuddered to think of the consequences. Tim wondered, are there Hospice programs everywhere? It was started in England and it has become a life saver ever since for thousands of people. Tim knew, even then, that his wonderful Millie was dying, and all he could do, day by day, was to sit by her bedside and watch her die, a little bit each day. And he cried. Tim was all man, but when you have to sit by her side, and watch her die a little bit each day, and you can't do a thing about it but watch, it will get to you, even if you're the strongest person in the world. That is the way God wanted it to be. And all Tim could do right at this minute was to cry his eyes out and pray to his Heavenly Father to bless him in his misery and let him endure, and take away the pain from Millie, as he knew she was in great pain from this dread disease.

And, Tim remembered being told how little Millie was so nice to older people. Even to the mailman, as he delivered the mail to their home each day. "Mr. Mail man, can I take the mail in to Mama?" "Of course, you can, Millie, you live here." And so it went with all adults who visited them. Millie didn't have to be told how to act. She learned her lessons well in Sunday School. Everyone remarked how well behaved she was, and always welcomed her into their homes knowing she behaved better than their own kids. Tim remembered how Ina had reacted when she first saw Millie after her ordeal. It hit Ina like a bombshell. Millie was still bleeding from her terrible tragedy from the village punk. Ina gave Millie a good sponge bath, and dreaded to think what Stan would do when he came home from his hard work in the fields. Stan came home from his work about 6:30, tired to the bone, and under orders from the Army doctors to take it easy or suffer greater pain from his ordeal in the war with the grenade exploding in his back.

As usual, Stan made a big deal out of coming home to his wife at the end of each day's hard work, and Ina loved every minute of it. Stan was her man, and she was so proud of the way he held up under all that pain. He never complained about his pain, but Ina knew he was in intense pain most of the time from having to wear his back brace so tight. Wars. Who needs them? The big shots need them, and the power hungry men needed them both for power and to lord it over other people whether it be for good or evil, they didn't seem to care. Ina decided to broach the subject of moving to Stan before he had a chance to really relax. "Stan, have you ever thought about moving away from here? I mean, we've been here quite a while, and your dad has never asked you for a nickel, and quite rightly we do owe him for staying here in their home without paying him anything, although you do more than your share in the fields." "Yes, Ina, I have thought about it. But, where could we go?" "Well", she said, "maybe we could go to Long Beach in California. Uncle Roe has a big manufacturing plant and he has asked us repeatedly to come out any tine we want to," "Well, maybe we can give it a little thought." Tim remembered how Millie's mother and dad had lingered over this subject for several weeks before making a decision and then the deciding factor was the awful way little Millie's body had been torn and mutilated, and not being able to do anything about it legally or medically. And this devastated Stan.

Tim's memory came rushing back. Horrible, as it was. And leaving his beautiful wife, Millie, at the mercy of time and the wrath of God. Oh, yes. He knew God would not let anything this horrible happen to one of His own creations without doing something about it. No question about it even though they were no longer in Payson, Utah. Sodom and Gomorrah, all rolled into one. Why? The Good Book says (paraphrased) "Suffer the little children to come unto me?" And why does this seem to be important? God said it, Tim believes it and that's that. Ask Tim> OK. Tim remembers a Letter he saw from Stan to uncle Roe, and it was to the point. One line said, "We are deeply grateful that you want us to come to Long Beach, and we are leaving soon. Please let us earn our bread as it says in our church teachings. We would then be most happy," And so it went. Roe was even happier to be able to help one of his own. That was the kind of man he was, and would ever be.

After a short time they soon learned Ina was allergic to the oil fields nearby. My, my, one set-back after another. But when you come from great stock, as were the people who settled the Salt Lake region, they were used to baffling odds, and they had the background to prove it. Tim had to smile in the middle of his thoughts about the early settlers if his valley, and felt that he had truly married into one fine family. Early history books and documents from the Fertile Crescent delineated how man in his early days had to earn his bread the hard way, and had to learn how to construct shelters for their growing families, and Tim felt somewhat akin to that type of life, and that early man, in history documents, were referred to as being in the building trades, stone masons, building masons, such as Joseph and his carpenter son, Jesus, who insisted that John the Baptist baptize Him, and how they got along so well, they, being called operative masons since they did the work, they decided to organize a fraternal nighttime meeting to discuss ways and means to live better lives, and called their organization "speculative masons."

And Tim reflected on some of the other organizations which also sprang up, and among them was such jealousy that it exists today. Practically all of it is pure baloney. Catholics have never said they would burn crosses on the foreheads of those who didn't join their church, it is pure nonsense. Baptists have had their share of bigotry, all nonsense. And so with Nazarenses, all baloney. And Tim had to smile at some of the outlandish jealousies surrounding the Mormon people. At the time of the Mexican War, there was no law regulating the number of wives or husbands people might have, and this covered all churches and all people. As the war took a heavy toll on the men who were killed in battle and made quick widows and orphans out of those left behind, the government turned its political head the other way so that what men were left here, regardless of church affiliation, were permitted to marry more than one woman to keep her and the orphans from starving to death. After a suitable time, the practice was then declared to be outlawed and all churches accepted the edict. Some individuals decided to ignore the edict, Tim was flabbergasted to learn all this but decided he had now learned something from history after all. Cults? No But some people still like to ignore truth and let their jealousy dictate bigotry at its worst. Hm, hm.

CHAPTER 8

While Tim is torturing himself unwittingly by reviewing in his mind some of the things that have brought this ugly situation this far, the District Attorney and Chief of Police have just completed a meeting in the City Hall that, if brought to fruition, will have far reaching effects on law enforcement in general and on juvenile rape in particular. They both agreed on a number of subjects that have plagued law enforcement for years and brought nothing but criticism from the general public and they wanted these to be eliminated completely if possible.

They both agreed this was going to be next to impossible. Who could accomplish such a Herculean task and tie together all the loose ends to make the endeavor a cost efficient task force. Task force? The mere thought of the words sent chills up and down their spines, and made them wonder if they were, indeed, going in the right direction. Both executives held meetings in their individual departments to see if any new ideas might come forth. The police chiefs secretary playfully suggested that if anyone could pull off such a wild and wooly project it would have to be fishermen since they were the greatest liars in the world anyway, and who better to that than Bob Bertacelli, their own ace detective, and Jim 2nd, retired police detective, first class, who was now bringing in the bad guys for the DA.

Everybody got a big laugh out of that, until the Chief, in his native wisdom, turned and looked directly at his secretary, who was taking down notes in short hand, and said in a quiet voice, "Now, wait just a dadgum minute. Let's think about that. We don't question the ability of those two characters to lie to such a degree they would have you believe their coffee cup was the Holy Grail. And you would probably believe it, too.

"Let's have some ideas on how we could go about this in an intelligent manner." And all the time Bob Bertacelli was trying his best to slide under his desk, unsuccessfully. "Chief," began one rookie who was in hopes of attracting power attention to his superb ability to bring forth intelligent ideas, "I believe you have hit on the one thing that has escaped all the rest of us." The Chief immediately expanded his chest at such a wonderful suggestion. But in all fairness, the chief didn't get his job by polishing apples and running after another cup of hot coffee for the governing board which chooses the hierarchy to run the police department. No. He actually got the job by doing better detective work than anyone else, and never complaining. He was really a credit to the department and the crown jewel of the city fathers who always looked to him for improvements, and they got them.

"Bob," began the Chief, "do you think Jim would go along with this idea? That is, if we could convince the DA that these two fine, upstanding detectives were the only two hard working officers that could successfully bring this difficult task to a close?" "Well," said Bob, "Tim is smarter than Bob and I would want him to take the lead in this case." While Bob was trying to weasel out of being the lead man, Jim was replying to the DA, "Sir, between the two of us, Bob is the smarter, and I would feel better if he could be appointed to that position."

Both men respected each other to such a degree that they offered the other as being smarter. Than they both had the exact IQ, both had excellent training as detectives, and they worked together so closely, you could never know which one had come up with the pearl of great price. So, the chief immediately got down to business in laying out the master plan and letting the two fishermen fill in the details. So as not to alert outside ears, the meeting was held behind closed doors, with only the Chief, and the two famous liars were in attendance, and that was the way they wanted it.

No one in either department was jealous of the two fishermen. It was just too big for the average detective to handle, and they knew it. Jim was allowed to let his father, Tim, know they were on to something big, but that was all. The two men were on gratis leave immediately, which made the hackles on both necks stand on end. They knew this mission, if successful, would hit the news media like Little Jack Horner sitting in the corner, and raising his hand with two fingers held on high not knowing the teacher was out in the hallway trying to get the attention of the handsome football coach, who, in turn, had been after the school secretary, who, well, anyway, off they went into what was soon to be, perhaps, either oblivion or fame.

The Chief and DA jointly signed a document to the Governor of Utah, asking for his or her permission to open a case that had been closed for years. The governor, a cousin of Senator Oren Hatch, first checked with the senator to see if there might be any repercussions to his permit, and was assured there would not be, since Sen. Hatch was one of the most highly respected men in Washington.

In due time, Bob, the appointed driver of the unmarked police car, and a former Indy driver, crossed the border into the great state of Utah, turned to Tim, and asked, "Want to drive by the Temple and go up to the top of the hill where Brigham Young looked out of the rear of the wagon, where his aids had tried to make him comfortable after his sickness ordeal, saw all this beautiful valley, and made the famous announcement, THIS IS THE PLACE." "Bob, you have been reading books, again, haven't you? Yes, I think that is permissible." And with a little grin, said, "And don't be so smug showing off your culture." Which brought a big smile to Bob's face, as they both enjoyed needling each other good naturedly.

And to the top of the hill they went. No sooner than they had stopped their car, got out to enjoy the natural beauty of the scene, than a highway patrolman pulled in right behind them, so they couldn't get out if they had to. "All right, fellas, didn't you see the sign that says, NO PARKING.?" "Yes, we did, officer; but we're from out of state," offered Bob, "and it's my fault. I've read in my history books about this place and I couldn't resist trying to be in the same spot as Brigham Young." "Are you referring to my great, great grandfather?" asked the trooper. And this caused both Bob and Tim to jerk their heads around to take a good look at temporary highway patrolmen, Steve Young, who broke out in the loudest laugh he had had all day. "Look, I radioed ahead and was told to give you guys full cooperation on anything you wanted, but I just couldn't resist a little fun." Bob looked at Steve and said, "Oh, if only you had a football in your hands right now?" And that caused Steve and Bob to give each other a big bear hug, with Tim waiting his turn.

Then Steve asked them, "Just what is your mission here, anyway. No one will tell me." "We can't, either, right now, but I'm sure we will later on.." offered Jim. "And knowing your morals as well as we do, you will be most welcome to our mission." Steve asked them, "Where are you staying while you're here?" "We don't know, yet. We just got here," from Bob. "No problem," said Steve. And he yanked out his phone and said the magic words that got Bob and Jim a place to stay as long as they needed it.

Steve said, "Here is my phone and home phone. Call me anytime I can help." And off he went in his little white wagon. With a wave of his hand he was out of sight. What a guy. He was better looking in person, both thought. And he was.

After conferring about the time of day, they decided to sack out for a brief nap, and then go to dinner. What's this, asked Bob to himself? No coffee listed on the room menu. No drinks? Oh, I remember, now. Mormons believe in the "word of wisdom" and, so help me, that sounds like good advice to me. So, while I am here, I will see if I can live without caffeine, and I don't use booze, anyway. So, there.

And they both drifted. Tomorrow is another day to dreamland. Tomorrow is another day.

CHAPTER 9

He had never heard this sound before and sincerely hoped he would never hear it again. He never had time to pray, but he did, anyway. "Oh, my Heavenly Father, Ruler of the Universe, in Thy Name, I pray that Millie will live. I need her so." Millie had just emitted a scream so loud, and so ugly, that Tim must have almost jumped clear out of bed. As Tim reached for her to see what had caused her to scream like this, his hand came away bloody, with blood all over Millie and the bed. Tim immediately reached for the phone beside the bed and dialed 9-1-1. He was almost incoherent but managed to get the information to the operator who had the ambulance on the road within less than a minute. Tim had never heard a blood curdling scream like that before in his entire life, but he heard this one. A horrible dream.

CHAPTER 10

While Bob and Jim are motoring into the Salt Lake Valley, just prior to the intersection that leads to Payson, Dr. Kelly and Dr. Mark are gathering their team together to map their next move in the careful analysis of Millie's precious moments in her quest for maintaining some son of life and the next addition of blood to give her tender body more flexibility than it had up to this moment. Her breathing seems to have leveled off slightly, and her pulse is more regular than before. Maybe there's hope, after all. Do doctors pray for their patients? Yes, they do. Ask any doctor. What a woman this Millie is. She has gone through more that she ought to, and still is hanging on to life. Wanda, one of the smartest ladies in the medical secretaries office, brought Dr. Kelly the latest figures on the intake of blood and the accurate information that accompanies the report. You want excellence in reporting, you want Wanda. She makes all the doctors look good. And the report she just handed Dr. Kelly was the one he needed drastically and right now. After discussing the report with Dr. Mark and the rest of the team, their next steps were clear, and they immediately started in the final steps in Millie's recovery.

Now the waiting begins. The internal organs told them the story they did not want to hear. As Dr. Kelly had previously mentioned to Dr. Mark, this frail creature must have been viciously raped at the tender age of five or six, and never had medical attention immediately following the attack. Why? Payson Medical Clinic had no record of any such occurrence at that period in time. Why not? No time to wander in circles now, the immediate course to take now is the saving of a precious life. Five more hours of tedious surgery before the sweat soaked doctors lay down their instruments, and gave a tremendous sigh of relief, and almost dropped to the floor in exhaustion. Millie had not opened her eyes since she had been admitted to the ER, and Dr, Kelly was beginning to get a little worried. Just then, Dr. Mark said, "Hold on. I just saw a flicker in her right eye." This brought the whole team to attention, as they crowded around the operating table with little silent prayers. Of course, they do. Doctors are human, just like anyone else. You wouldn't want a doctor with a knife in his hand that didn't know how to pray, and he's coming straight at you with a mask on his face?

More waiting. But doctors are used to this. They don't like it, but are used to it. Tim had conked out two hours ago, and this bit of news brought him to life instantly. He had already cried all his tears out, but like any good man, had a reserve that told his Maker he was ready to give his life any time to save that of his beloved. He was trembling so badly the doctor suggested to the attending nurse that she give Tim a shot to keep him in the land of the living, and she did. A slight noise came from the throat of Millie that got the immediate attention of the group, and they were mesmerized to the spot. No more noises, but Millie's breathing did seem to be steadying off. The air surrounding the lady on the operating table seemed to be filled with electricity, and the entire team responded with nervous energy showing, just mentally urging the patient to respond with sustained life.

While all this was going on, Bob and Tim entered the little city of Payson, where Tim's parents inhabited long before he was a twinkle in his dad's eye. To the uninitiated nothing had changed in this town since Noah made a pair of oars for his tug boat. The city hall was the stand-out building, so it wasn't hard to find. Parking was not a problem, either. No meters, no red curbs, no parking signs and no restrictions for parking. Well, some things are still good to see. As they entered the building over wooden steps, they were eyed with suspicion by a single lounger in a wooden chair just inside the door, who immediately challenged their existence, and pointed to a seven star badge hanging ominously from his shirt pocket. "What do you guys want? This is a peaceful city, and I intend to keep it that way?"

CHAPTER 11

So pulling out of the parking lot was not as secret as they would have liked, but Tim and Bob had to proceed anyway. Their first stop was at a gas station to fill up. They didn't know just how much idle of the engine was going to be involved so not to take any chances. Why? Religious people called the action "blessings,' women called the action "intuition." Men called the action, "logic." Whatever it was cops had to have it, or they could be in jeopardy most of the time. A feeling? A vision? Joseph Smith, Jr. had it, and called it a vision. It worked, so who cares what it is or was?

Out to the boonies went Tim and Bob. Was anyone following? No, why not? Somehow, Willie had dropped a load of lumber on the highway, and it was blocked for hours. Willie was happy as though he had good sense. Had he lost his marbles? No. Not Willie, nor Ben. They knew what they were doing. So, all is well, so far. Next phase was to turn around and see the Mayor, and give him the official papers from their bosses in Santa Rosa.

As they walked in to the mayor's office, the secretary smiled at them and said, oh, yes, you wanted to see the mayor. And into the inner sanctum she went. Coming back out, she curtsied and said, "His Honor, the Mayor, will see you now," And she held open the door for the two California warriors to do their thing. Hiram 2nd, a lawyer, was the newly elected mayor, and was most affable to these two who were on a secret mission, so to speak. "Now, don't be alarmed. This is a small town, and news travels fast. Do you have your letter of introduction?" "Yes, we have, your honor." said Tim. "I'll go get it. It's in the glove compartment. Be right back." When he shut the door, Bob, the ever nice returned missionary, tried to make small talk by asking the mayor if he felt that he, Bob, looked like Clark Gable? He said women were always telling him that.

The mayor, noncommittally tried to look straight at Bob, and Bob tried to be equally bland, both looking like they had just seen two worms in mating season, and that was the way they were when Tim brought the papers to the Mayor to approve. "OK, your honor. Here are the papers." Grateful for the timely interruption, the mayor deftly flourished his signature on the affidavit, and handed it back to Tim, "here you are."

After some small talk, the two detectives got into their police limousine and headed toward their destination. On the way, Bob broke out in his best voice, singing "The Barber of Seville" much the same as if he were the star of the San Francisco Opera, and about as classy. This serenade was not lost on Tim who sang The Merchant of Venice with the same gusto, and this duo pleased Bob immensely.

"Bob," asked Tim, "are you sure we're on the right road? We just went through Logan. I think that is still in Utah, but that sign over there said "Welcome to Wyoming." "Oh, my goodness. Are you sure? Say, I heard Wyoming was going to have a very strong football team this year. Did you hear that? Those guys are big and raw boned. If they play BYU for the conference title this year I want to see that. Man, that ought to be a real humdinger."

"Bob," persisted Jim, "don't you think we might ought to turn around, or at least ask someone where the heck we are?" "Oh, sure. Let's do that." At the next service station they filled up the tank and asked where they were "Hey, man, if you don't know, I don't want to spoil your fun. But if I were you, I'd call my wife and tell her I might just be two hours late for dinner tonight." That did it. Bob and Tim got back in their joy wagon and headed back to Utah, from whence they came.

As they went through the check station, the attendant reminded them that "they were in the great state of Utah, and that all this baloney about plural marriages being approved was all hog wash, and that Joseph Smith, Brigham Young, George Q. Canon, and many other earlier settlers were indeed members of the Masonic Lodge, contrary to what you might have heard. It is not a cult, and I am a proud member."

So much for that. Now to find rural route — what was it? Oh, there it goes over that way. "Now, we're not lost, Tim. I knew we were on the right road all along. I just wanted to make you think that." My, there sure is a lot of sweat on Bob's forehead. Wonder why? Now to keep track of the miles on the odometer so we will know where that home is. Hm, hm.

One mile. Two miles. Three miles. Oh, please, dear me. Don't do it, Bob pleaded to himself, Somebody heard him. A big yellow sign near the seven mile marker said, ETERNAL HOME Your Next Home is Heaven and under all this it says, Do Not Pick Up Hitch Hikers.

Bob's eyes misted over, His own mother is in one of these Alzheimer's Homes. But coming here was for a more sinister reason. They were told by a reliable source in Payson, that this was their destination, and they would indeed find the object of their long and arduous journey. By now, both men were almost wringing with the sweat of anticipation of the fulfillment of their dreaded mission. Both men, without either being aware of the other's hope for failure, knew they had to proceed to the end of their mission.

This was a home for Alzheimer's disease patients. The more dangerous ones. The ones who were diagnosed, some many years ago, with the dread disease from which there was no return. Only death was the release valve for all who entered here. And only the most violent ones were here, or were coming here. There was one patient who was hated above all the rest, and who had the civilian record of being the meanest, hardest, cruel and most ruthless of all the rest put together. And this record was the same in this institution as in civilian life before coming here.

And this was the man Bob and Tim came to see. He refused to give his name even before he was beyond recall. Now it was too late. He was known both far and wide as Bob the Puke, sometimes known as Bob the Punk.

Yes. He was still alive. The administrator believed him to be in his mid nineties. His age was not a barrier to his personality. He had killed and mangled several patients here before he could be stopped and placed in solitary bondage. His pride and joy was a little girl playing jacks with the other little girls on the sidewalk in front of their home many years ago. His memory was razor sharp on this one. Why? No one knows. That's the way Alzheimer' s is.

You can remember some better than others. Your memory plays tricks on you. There are times when you won't even remember your own name, where you live, any information at all about themselves, denial of any or all information relative to good or evil, you will cuss like a sailor from long past memories, and you won't know why, you will deny everything, you won't even know those who have been the closest to you even for all your life, you will equate loved ones with the most horrible of all actions or crimes, you will deny your own husband, or wife, to be close to you or to even sleep in the same bed, or if you do let them, you will deny their closeness to you for fear they are the ones that are bad to you. In other words, you, the caregiver, will be hurt by them so deeply, it could even take years for you to recover.

You must remember, they are themselves in deep pain most of the time, and caring for them will hurt you deeper than you could ever know. Grieving? Yes. You will grieve. And grief will not go away as you wish it to. You will grieve in several ways different ways, and at times around other people, when you wish you couldn't, it is most embarrassing, as you cannot know just what word or words might trigger your grief, and you cannot do a thing about it. The toughest, hard-bitten person will break down and cry like a baby at tunes when you wish you were in the middle of the desert by yourself, Grieving knows no bounds, you are it, and accept it.

And Bob the Punk? He openly brags about his trophy, that little girl, who blossomed into one of the most beautiful women alive and married the man her mother always said she should try to find, and one who would accept her rape as a little girl, playing jacks on the sidewalk, as part of his mission in life and to take care of her always until he dropped, regardless of anything else, and her name was LaVey, and his name was Jim, the author of this book.

CHAPTER 12

Alzheimer's disease is one of the deadliest diseases to ever hit mankind. It is so unpredictable as to all who are so unfortunate as to be victims of it, so says the information on the bulletin board of the Home. When dealing with the patients who are afflicted with the disease be very careful in your actions and reactions with them. Your own emotions are most important. If you are happy, show it. If the patient does something that displeases you, let him or her know that in whatever form you feel is necessary, anger, sadness, whatever is the norm. The bulletin is very explicit in keeping the visitor up to date on the latest information pertaining to good relationships with the loved one.

"Tim," started Bob, "what do you think we should do? That man may be in his nineties, and according to the history here pertaining to him, he is the punk that mutilated your mother and caused her to almost not conceive you, to have an abortion that was very painful to her, and to put ten years difference between you and your sister, and end her quest for more children, and according to the medical board, chaired by Dr. John Shrum at the hospital (any relation), this SOB deserves to feel the wrath of my six inch right that put a number of boxers to dreamland, so why can't I just take one little bitty chop on his prominent chin? Now answer me that?"

Tim thought, how in the name of holy thunder did this wonderful friend of mine ever keep that much characterization together in one thought without blowing a gasket? But what he answered was, "Bob, if that was the approved method of dealing with law breakers like him, knowing that Dr. Shrum's report listed his mutilation of my mother as the most probable cause of her brain explosion, do you think I would let you get first crack at him?" And this rather lengthy reply hit Bob right in his gizzard and made him laugh till he almost cried.

Both men felt the same way apparently. This dread disease can be triggered by a number of ways, it seems. No one really knows for sure, but a doctor's examination of a woman can pretty much pinpoint cruelty and viciousness on the part of some sex crazed monster like Bob the Punk. All this, on the Home's bulletin Board, to inform visitors with standard information for their official uses.

Bob and Jim just stood there digesting the information from the bulletin board, and making notes in their official police files, until the Home's secretary informed them they will have to leave for the day, and return tomorrow if they like. Tim turned to Bob and said, "I have all the information I need. How about you?" "Yeah, I don't need any more, but I'd still like to take just one little poke at that (blank's) chin."

On the way back to their hotel, they were silent, digesting all the information they had taken on Bob the Punk, in general, and Alzheimer's disease in particular.

On yelling "hi" at Willie, he stopped them and said he had a telephone message for them. It was in crypt, so Willie was wide eyed to know what it said. Naturally, Bob volunteered to do the honors. "Willie," he said in all seriousness, "the Police Chief is so pleased with our report, he said we were up for the highest award ever to be bestowed on a public servant. Isn't that just like him? He really went all out with the Santa Rosa board to get this for us." "Hey, that's great, Bob. Now how long did you have to ponder to come up with that baloney?" This made all three of them bust their sides laughing. They knew the crypt was secret.

So, like good little boys, after a hard day at the office, they decided to sack out till dinner time.

Next morning bright and early at 9:30 (that's early for cops on special duty) they decided to roll out of bed and get crackin'. Jim was the first to pick up the special folder for the second leg of their mission. What they had so far was enough for a full report for both the Chief and DA, and to make them look good. Now for the cream on the cake.

Bob came over and picked up the pages as Jim finished with them, and as he read, his emotions showed. "Tim, now we got to go to North Lake Tahoe, and try to find a needle in a haystack." "Tell me about it. But we got to try."

Breakfast was consumed mostly in silence. The cute little waitress brought them their usual cup of hot Sanka, and hot, buttered French Toast, the morning news tabloid, and let them go at it. Not just cute, but smart as a whip. She gave them complete silence while she could see they were seriously into their thing, their mission.

When they were finished she gave them both a hug, a little peck on the cheek and wished them both good luck on their second leg of their mission. "Yes," she confessed, "I knew what your mission was and also your second mission. This is a little town, and we detest anyone who harms little girls, and big ones, too, for that matter, the weaker sex, you know." What a wife she is going to make some lucky man, Tim thought.

As they pulled out of Payson, Bob said, "I saw you slip that waitress a twenty." Tim replied, "Yes, and I saw you slip her another twenty. How did you know she was Steve Young's little sister?" "Elementary, my dear friend. I saw an autographed picture on her desk that said, LUV YA, SIS"

Bob glanced over at Tim while they were mobiling down the freeway, "Hey, what's that package? I never saw you buy anything"" "I didn't." "Well, what is it?" As Tim took his time unwrapping one of the packages, he hummed a familiar tune, "Home on the Range" until Bob said, "That's awful." And Tim handed one of the unwrapped items to Bob, and it said, "Bob, thanks for being nice to my baby sister, Steve.

"I got one, too," "You know, Tim, that Steve is OK But when did he see us?" "His sister said they stopped by for just a minute en route to Denver." "Well, son of a gun".

"Hey. Wanna stop for lunch in Winnemucca? And maybe throw in a couple of nickels?" "Sure. Claudia gave me a roll of nickels, just in case."

So, in the den of iniquity they went, nickels burning the palms of their hands. "Wow" shouted Bob above the noise of the casino. They had to look all over the place before they found three nickel machines. Prosperity, you know. Bob put in one after the other, and when he got down to four nickels he said, "What the heck. Might as well be a big spender, so he put in all four nickels and hit three sevens, starting to turn away, until he saw what happened, and then he yelled for the money changer to pay him off.

Tim had already hit 50 nickels, and wisely put them in his pocket to give to Claudia to make her happy, too. "Hey. Let's grab a bite to eat while we're here." "OK," said Tim. So into the bar and grill they went and as they crossed into the grill a lady was also leaving a one armed bandit and crossed herself with a look Heavenward, as if to say, Don't blame me, Lord. The Devil made me do it.

CHAPTER 13

As Bob and Jim came out of the casino to get into their assigned car, they noticed a small boy across the street saluting the American Flag and saying something. As if their minds were connected, both men automatically went across the street and watched the boy finish his recitation of the Pledge, gave it a snappy salute, and deftly put his right arm smartly to his side. Amazed at what they had just witnessed, Jim asked the youngster if he did this everyday. "Darn tootin' I do. Anything wrong with that?" In unison, both men denied anything wrong. Then Bob said, "Aren't you afraid someone might jump on you for saying the Pledge on school grounds?"

"Let 'em jump. I'll do it anyway." "Why are you so touchy about this," asked Tim. "Because I am part Choctaw Indian, and I am more American than you are, that's why." Bob asked, "Would Apache Indian be acceptable?" "Darn tootin' it would. That's American, Isn't it?" "Darn tootin' it is," mimicked Bob. "And how about you, copper?" asked the lad. "Now how did you know we are police officers," asked Jim. "I saw your car, and my daddy taught me how to spot police cars, marked or not," "You got a smart daddy."

"As far as the court goes, they got to follow some silly rules to make some people happy," continued the lad. "Indians were here before anyone else was. That what they taught us in our native schools, before we had to attend public schools. We were even taught there was a man with long beard teaching us things that they don't teach in public schools. They called Him 'THE GREAT WHITE FATHER" and He liked that because He said that was what He was. We still refer to Him as The Great White Father. Don't make no difference where you are, it's still the same name. Man. He sure must have gotten around a lot." And this made both men smile. They knew the history behind most of this.

"Would you like to say the Pledge for us, just to make sure you have the right words?" "Sure. Here goes" And he proudly straightened up, his shoulders square, head and bearing that of a trained soldier, and in a strong voice, said- "I pledge allegiance to the Flag of the United States of America, and to the Republic for which it stands, one nation under God, with liberty and justice for all." And he gave the flag another snappy salute and whipped his arm to his side, and with a big smile, turned to us and asked, "Is that OK?" With eyes slightly misty, both men grabbed the youngster and said "More than OK. It's the best we ever heard" And that really pleased the boy, as he had just demonstrated that his age group was smart alter all.

Tim said, "Give me your name, and I'll 1 give you an. autographed copy of this book" So the lad wrote his name in the book, Freddie Reagan 3rd, and received a copy of The Umbrella Theory, for which he was most grateful. After a fond farewell, the men mounted their mechanical steed, and off to the races they went.

As they neared the Nevada border, Bob waved a friendly goodbye to no one in particular, and took the south road that led them to North Lake Tahoe, and to the second leg of their mission. "Man. This country is beautiful," mused Bob. And Tim agreed. He had been here a number of times with his dad, Tim, and his grandfather, Ben, and not caring whether or not they got a buck.

As the mountain road wound around curves and gullies, both men began to get just a little bit nervous. After all, their orders were .not to open their second mission envelope until they were in the parking lot of the North: Lake Tahoe Casino, so as not to alert their prey. After both men had memorized the name, description, and the other relevant information, they locked the papers in the glove compartment, for which there was only one key. Checking their pieces to make sure all was in working order, they shook hands, for they knew one, or both, might not come out of this alive.

Neither man drank hard stuff, so to make it seem like a routine one armed bandit call, they splashed a little Jim Beam on their shirts, and staggering slightly, started through the welcome doorway to possible oblivion. Just coming out were three of the hardest looking men ever to shoot six policemen and serial rape twelve under 11 young, defenseless girls, maiming three, and sexually mutilating the rest just for the fun of it. Face to face. What to do? "You make one move, and the four snipers right behind you are under orders to die first and ask questions later," this came out of the mouth of Tim, seconded by Bob.

"On the floor, face down, and do it right now, as my finger is twitching," from Bob, just twitching all over making his nervousness seem like he was ready to kill somebody, and the men thought it just might be them. Two off duty Truckee cops came up just then, identified themselves, and got the go ahead to draw their police .45's and cover the three killers, with even more nervousness than Bob showed.

Cuffing them was no problem at all. Real killers? Not when the kill might be them. They were more than glad to cooperate. The scene gave Tahoe the touch of realism they had all envisioned when they came in, Mow the customers were happy. They had seen the real thing. And to top it all off, some wise guy started the applause and the rest followed. Oh, well.

Out in the back seat of the specially equipped police car, the three desperadoes didn't seem so desperate, but that was all window dressing as the two highly trained police officers well knew. Bob kept messing with the butt of his police positive, and that just made the three hoods nervous as the enemy soldiers in the Philippines when General Macarthur said on no uncertain terms, "I'LL BE BACK", and he was. You just don't mess with finality.

The three hoods got nervous by the minute, since Bob kept looking back at them in the rear view mirror. Bob is one of the most ruggedly handsome, and hard looking men ever to put on a cop's tunic and give an innocent stare to a person with a guilty conscience. Just don't get him riled. Tim just loved it when Bob appeared to be nice. He just couldn't do it.

Two of the men decided to rankle Bob anyway, so they started singing "The Jailhouse Rock". They didn't know it was on Bob's all-time hate list, so when Bob stopped the car, they thought he wanted more so they really got into it. Bad move. In the first place, their voices were so awful, even termites in the forest left their hiding places and begged for asylum. And so it goes. Jim just sat there and laughed his head off when Bob said to the first thug he saw, "Stick your chin out a little farther. I don't like it, and I have every intention of changing it." "No, you don't," yelled the yellow belly. "You can't hit us when we are cuffed, and you know it." "Well, why don't I uncuff you?" "Bob, let the little (blank) alone. I may have to do the same to him. But we aren't supposed to." That brought a big raspberry from the thug to Bob, and brought a lump to the thug's chin. "Hey, no problem, Tim He just zigged when he should have zagged.", and Bob was happy.

As they passed Loomis, and Rocklin, they knew they were making good time going home. Jim got out his cell phone and dialed his dad's phone, but no answer. Must be out in the yard mowing it, even though his heart told him not to. Stubborn, and Tim grinned, just like me.

Pulling into the police parking lot in Santa Rosa, it seemed to these two warriors they had been gone forever, but it was only a few days. Jim had tipped off the chiefs secretary on the way, they would be coming in at about this time, and she, in turn, had told the chief and the visiting DA, as to the time. Bad move. This trip had national implications, because of the enormity of the crimes committed, and the far reaching effects of the two men involved. Cameras and microphones appeared like magic, and were strategically placed by the Chief and DA as to get the most efficient coverage. And they got it. TV stations all over the country had been told ahead of time what these two ace detectives were up to, and advertisers by the dozen were vying for space and time as though it were as big as the super bowl. It wasn't, of course, but the enormity of the mission, and the expert way it was handled by the DA and the Chief, not to mention the superb manner of execution by Bob and Tim, just made the whole thing explode like Santa Rosa had just discovered the Holy Grail.

And now, time for the participants to catch their breath while they still had some to catch.

CHAPTER 14

As the group headed to the city hall from the parking lot, one of the city's energetic employees pulled out a pad and started writing something on it. Tim noticed this and asked the man what he was doing. "I don't think it is any of your business what I'm doing, Buster, so get the holy heck out of my way before I throw you out." Bob was watching the whole thing with a big grin and wondered just what Tim was going to do.

Tim nonchalantly stepped on the man's toes and at the same time took the pad from his hands, and tore out the last entry that had Tim's name on it, and gave it to one of the senator's standing nearby, "Here you are, senator. Do you know what you can do with it?" The senator, fortunately, had a sense of humor, and called the attendant over and said, "Young man, if I were you I'd retreat as swiftly as I could. The man you just tried to intimidate could rip you to pieces, and throw the rest to the buzzards, if they would have it."

So, on to the waiting news media and the rest of the hot shots just waiting to get their mugs in the news and their names in big print, hopefully. Bob said something to Jim and took off running. This brought some mighty strong objections from the Washington delegation, and threats of all sorts of discipline they could throw at Bob.

Jim walked over to the apparent leader, and in spite of the DA's negative head shake, said in a steely voice with eyes to match, "Sir, you had no way to know about this, but that man's mother is in a special home for the Alzheimer' s patients, and he has been worried about her the whole trip, but man that he is, he made the trip anyway on orders from the Chief. My mother just died recently from the same disease, so I'm aware of the circumstances. Are we forgiven, Sir?"

The senator who had made the boo-boo apologized all over the place, and gave his secretary some quiet instructions, and with a head movement, she took off. That out of the way, the group moved on inside to the conference room where names were discreetly placed on each chair, the best chairs going to the highest rank, etc., When all of them were seated, with the Chief and DA at the head table, several court stenos assumed their places with their dresses appropriately at the usual level, just enough for the viewers to be properly distracted according to plan.

Bob came in and sat down beside Tim. The senator who had chastised Tim in the parking lot tried to make things calmer by leaning over and saying to Bob, "You've sure got a good partner there." To which Bob answered, "He's the best, and you'd better believe it. That's the way we both work."

In the group, near the front, sat the medical appointees who had been selected for the board, with Dr, John Shrum, as the chair. He was the medical expert on any phase of urology with his two specialty assistants. The guy really knew what he doing, alright. After the usual introductions had been made, the DA, acting as the lead, opened the meeting by special introductions of Tim and Bob, who were now the stars of the show, as it were.

"Ladies and gentlemen, let's not make a three ring circus of this. We had an opportunity to show the viciousness of the killer, Alzheimer' s Disease, which is spreading across America all too fast, and with the expert help of Dr. Shrum and his staff we have been able to solve the case in Utah which gained such nationwide attention about child abuse, which Dr. Shrum heatedly calls Eternal Rape, since it starts with a young child and systematically eats away at the brain all the child's life right on into eternity —" at which Dr. Shrum jumped to his feet and yelled, "Ladies and gentlemen that just makes me mad as hell that we can't do something about it. This case that Tim and Bob were assigned to investigate, is a prime example of a child being raped and mutilated at four or five, and carried that stigma and emotional hurt all her life, eating away at her brain, and nothing can be done about it, and her husband, Tim, crying desperately for help constantly, sitting by her bedside watching her die a little each day, with only the Hospice Program of Michael Poe, being the only source of help for this type of disease. I'm sorry to explode, but we've made the first real move with Tim and Bob, who also brought back three felons and their records of eternal rape hanging over their heads.

Silence. Then all of a sudden, everyone started talking at once, with the news media flashing their bulbs, and yelling their heads off at their cell phones. When order could finally be restored, and it took a while, Bob and Tim, along with Dr. Shrum, were literally besieged for information and knowledge of what they could do. Facetiously, Bob turned to Tim and said under his breath, 'SHOOT THE BASTARDS ON SIGHT' And this was the national headlines the next day. It also brought down the wrath of the Police Chief on Bob. As an aside the chief said, "you done good, Bob." Tim just sat there, tears running down his face, remembering how his mother looked three weeks before she died, as she lay on her deathbed, looking up at husband Tim, and asking, "Honey, am I going Home?" What could Tim say? "Yes, honey, I think so." And he stumbled over to a corner of the bedroom and cried like his heart was breaking. And it was.

Right now, Tim took Bob by the hand, and said, "Why don't we go see how your mother is doing? I know you love her, and you have a right to know." Bob never hesitated. "Let's go."

The chief saw them leave, but had the common sense to let them go. He knew where they were going anyway. Make no mistake about it. He never made chief just by picking his nose.

As Bob and Tim entered the bedroom of his mother, her face lit up like a roman candle. "My baby, my baby." Bob didn't like to be called a baby, but this was different. Fortunately Bob's mother still knew him. But he knew the time was coming when she wouldn't know him or anyone else. And he dreaded the thought of it. As though Tim read Bob's mind, and that wasn't too far fetched, as they both worked together like two peas in a pod, Tim grabbed Bob's hand and said, "Bob, I'm with you all the way. When the going gets tough, just remember, I'm here. Call on me."

Bob just nodded. When you're choked up, that's all you can do. But that's enough. After the usual half hour visit, they finally left. Before they got to the door, his mother was asleep. Nothing was said on the way back to the office. Since both men's offices were in the same building, they bade farewell and went back to their desks and tried to look busy, but it just wouldn't come. Finally, Jim went into the chiefs office, after the mandatory OK from the secretary, which was a formality, and the usual "go right in."

""Now, Tim, tell me the truth. Did Bob earn his bread on this trip?" "Yes, he did, chief I'm not lying. I know I don't work for you anymore, but I fully respect you, and even when I did work for you before I retired and went to work for the DA, I always laid it on the line" "I know that, Tim. I was just pulling your leg."

The chief remembered Tim's reactions when someone mentioned his mother, and he said, "Tim, there ain't nothing to do right now, so why don't you take the day off? I'll make it right with the DA, We do this all the time?" "Hey, thanks, chief" The chief looked down at the little signs under the glass on his desk. One said BE REASONABLE. DO IT MY WAY. Another said, REASON? THERE AIN'T NO REASON. IT'S COMPANY POLICY Another sign read, LOVE YOUR ENEMY. IT'LL DRIVE HIM CRAZY And the chief smiled at the good humor, and said, "Ain't it the truth."

Next morning, the chief and DA got together for coffee and donuts, and talked about what Dr. Shrum had said. He was right, angry as a jilted old maid after being rejected by a bum passing through town, but Dr, Shrum had the credentials to do something about it. And the chief and DA wanted to take advantage of his expertise on the subject. There was no one better qualified to chair such a commission so the two decided they would broach the subject to the good doctor, and see what his reaction would be. Strike while the iron is hot, that sort of thing.

"Dr. Shrum, this is the DA. Thanks for taking my call. Have you got a minute?" "Sure. What did I do? Commit a crime while I was sleeping in the park?" "No," laughed the DA. "The chief and I have a plan and an idea we want to talk to you about." "OK. "I'm listening." "John, may I call you John?" "Sure. I was born with it, so go ahead." "Well," started the DA. "We think that with your expertise and experience, you would be the logical choice to chair a commission regarding the many cases of Alzheimer's disease right here in California,"

"Well, now, that sounds like it could wind up being bigger than all of us put together." "And it very well could. But I think we all agree that it has merits to burn. "I agree.
So let's give it some more thought." "OK by me," said Dr. Shrum.

CHAPTER 15

"But first, let's go see what Judge Wilma has to say to the escaped child rapist we brought in." "Yeah, let's do that," said Bob. "I hope he wants to act up. I need to powder his little nose with my big No, 12's," And the meaning left no doubt as to what he wanted to do.

From time to time, Tim kept reflecting on his beautiful wife, Millie about how she was feeling, and if there was anything he could do to ease the constant pain of her Alzheimer's. He had known for sometime, now, that she didn't know him from Adam, but accepted him as being something that she couldn't do anything about.

Dr. John Shrum looked at Dr. Mark Johnson, who, in turn, arched his eyebrows as high as he could get them and started grabbing a notepad to take notes. Dr. Shrum motioned for the attendant to turn on the tape, and for the steno to start taking notes. He didn't want anything to be missed that might give the defense a ladder for a new trial. Even though Millie was quite young when this rape occurred, there were times when she showed signs of dementia or having hallucinations and that might just be enough for the defense to ask for either trial or at least an extension of this one.

At this particular state of Millie's affliction, she had been having bouts of cursing Tim at night for about a month, but he had kept this to himself as he didn't even want anyone to know about it. Once he asked Millie where she had heard these words (all the time knowing she was not herself, but in a world all her own), and she had told him she heard the girls in her class in high school use these gutter words. This only lasted a month, so it seemed best to keep it to himself.

Alzheimer's is a strange disease. It affects each person differently. As soon as you think you have enough information to give a definition of it, something else pops up to throw out that window. Male or female, makes no difference, and that is what makes it so hard to treat. There are more experts in this field than Carter has fleas.

There was an old man sitting by Tim who kept trying to talk to both of them, and they were trying to hear the testimony against the rapist they had brought in. He said he knew all about the rape of Millie. That brought Tim upright, and he practically shouted "Why didn't you do something about it at the time?" "Young man, I am 96 years old, and how I got this old was by keeping my mouth shut. That Bob the Punk would as soon cut my throat as look at me.

"I figger I might be safe to talk to you now, you packin' a gun and all. You even got a tin badge, so there. Am I right? Or are you just makin' believe?" "No, you are right. But that is not in our jurisdiction, we are just criminal investigators, but we can act as material witnesses if you will give us a statement after this trial is over with." "If I last that long. I ain't gettin' any young, you know."

Time for a lunch break. So Bob and Tim hit the lunch wagon first, naturally, curled up in the court's lawn chairs and ravenously ate their ptomaine tommie sandwiches, and hot so-called coffee. After lunch, they decided to look up the old man and see if he had any more info that might help in their report to the Chief and DA. He gave them the name of a new deputy in Payson who was a little skittish about digging out the old files, but jumped like a frog burping up flies when they assured him of national attention in their report. "Yeah, here it is. The report says, and I quote, 'On (such and such a date) it was reported to us by some little girls that they were playin' jacks on the sidewalk when Bob the Punk took one of the little girls, Millie, to his house and gave her some cookies. When she came back runnin', she had blood all over her and she was cryin' and went into her own house. That's all we know.', So, that's about all we have on it

"Call me. back in two weeks. I may have more for you." Tim said, "Thanks, deputy. We will do just that." "Well, well," said Tim. "Now we know for sure, that old man at the Alzheimer's home was the culprit."

They decided to give this information to the Chief and DA right away, so off they went to turn in their reports. While Millie was receiving expert care from the ace caregivers, The Hospice Nurses, getting her medicine, paid for by the Hospice People, and her daily bath, the whole thing was being supervised by Michael Poe, the nurse in charge, you couldn't buy this service from anyone, but your contributions to them would certainly help them.

As Tim and Bob were contemplating their next move, Bob smiled, as only he can when he has a fly up his nose, so Tim asked him what was in his fragile mind. "Oh, I was just a thinkin' — what did you say?" Tim said, "Please tell me what you were thinkin'" "Oh, when my old man was on the force, he used to say, 'don't forget, son, you can get more confessions with a gun and a smile, than you can get with a smile." Tim just laughed, as he knew this was just an old joke, and not for real.

Tim thought back to their interview with the Alzheimer's rapist, when he, in his best off-the shoulder style, prodded the braggart to let loose with his hidden information, when he asked, "Oh, I'll bet you know all the secrets of how to get any woman to swoon over you, and then you get her in bed whether she wants to or not, right?" In his best shaky 96 year old voice, he bragged, "You got it right, son. I was a real dinger."

"And how about the little ones? You're so big and strong. Did you have any trouble with them?" "No. Not much. They were too afraid to move," Then Tim remembered Bob got into the act as he hated the very ground this old rapist walked on. "And they do anything you make them do?" "Now, you got it. I make 'em do it, and then they love it. I'm good, actually the best."

"I'll bet you remember all their names, too," coaxed Tim. "Oh, no. But I do remember one, cute legs, dark curly hair, snappy black eyes, great complexion, Mildred, or something like that" "Was it Millie?" asked Tim?" "Yeah, that's the one. I had to wreck her insides with my hands to make her mind. She was feisty, that one."

Bob and Tim both almost fell off their chairs at this outburst. They had their man, now. But what could they do, extradite a man, who, admittedly, raped a child 91 years ago? The court would laugh them out of the state. OK, they had done their job.

Should they have the old man sign a statement as to what he admittedly had done? It wouldn't hold up, and they knew it, but their first leg of the mission was done.

Back at the hospital, with Dr, Shrum's memory hard at work, he remembered how Dr. Patch had performed, what some called miracles, patient improvement against all odds, so he thought he might also be in a position to do similar treatment, as he dearly loved to treat his patients, and they loved him for it, no doubt about that. Well, why not? Wasn't a smile better than a frown? You bet your aunt Mamie's old broken girdle, it was.

"Millie," said Dr. Shrum, 'The head nurse tells me, they can't do anything more for you, but to give you what they call 'maintenance' which is next to nothing, which I regret, but which your attending doctor approved. So, we will call your husband and give him the news. I am aware he and his daughter had a hard time tasking care of you, but my hands are tied." About this time, Tim ran into Dr, Johnson in the hallway downstairs, who asked how Millie was. "Not good at all. And now, the nurses say they can't do anything more for her. Well, let me make it loud and clear. I don't blame you, you've done all you can, but I am going to take care of my wonderful wife until I drop." And both men departed peacefully.

Tears were brimming in Tim's eyes, as he knew what all this meant, that Millie was soon going Home to her Heavenly Father, and he, Tim couldn't do anything to help his wife. All he could do now was just sit by her side at home. day and night, and watch her die, a little bit each day, until her Heavenly Father calls for her. The only help he could get now, was the Hospice ladies, who gave his wife the best and finest care possible, and even asked Tim one day, why Millie was hanging on to life when she only had a few more days to live?

Tim asked, "What can I do? I love her and want to keep her as long as I can.?" The Hospice nurse admitted he was being normal, but the fact that he wanted to keep her was what was making her want to stay, even though her body functions had ceased to work, and she was just a vegetable, now. Just three days before she passed away, even though she had been unable to speak for ten days, she whispered to Tim in the middle of the night "I don't want to die."

He sat upright in the chair by her bed that he had used for three weeks as his bed, when he heard this, and tried to give her some water through a straw, she took some, and the Tim gave her a little Pepsi through a straw, for she loved it, and she gave him just the faintest of smiles for the Pepsi and closed her eyes. She was resting now, and Tim fell asleep.

Part Two

I DON'T WANT TO DIE
A Love Story

CHAPTER 1

It is possible that everyone, at one time or another, has expressed the feeling that they are having such a great life that they would like to stay that way forever. A natural feeling, one that creates a great desire to continue in the same way of life forever, yet they are fully aware this is impossible. The sky is blue, the weather is balmy, problems have passed you by, your loved one is absolutely great to you, your health is wonderful, money is flowing in like wine, the kids are doing great on their own, your future looks absolutely tremendous, not a flaw anywhere, your church services have all fallen into place, and there just doesn't seem to be anything to worry about. Well, what else could you wish for?

Why not start out at the beginning and let nature take it's course, as they say. "They", as you are aware of, takes a beating from all sides. So, what better way to begin this masquerade, than to say, "I remember when I was just about one and a half years old, I was playing out by the little pen where a small calf was inside the pen yelling his head off for some food. I didn't know how to handle this, but one of my sisters did. She let him out of the pen to eat some of the nice green grass, but instead he came straight at me and butted me a good one. Sure, I cried. I was expected to. It didn't hurt, but I cried, anyway. I remembered all that, but my sister said I was too young to remember those things. Maybe she is right. Quen sabe, as they say south of the border?

Memories. An odd section of the brain that stores all sorts of things. As time marches on, new jobs, and moving, were the vogue. Stories from the first person singular were changed from that phase to the third person singular to make things more palatable. And so we will fall in line with the story being told from the old phase to the third person singular. The great depression had its hold on almost everyone. Some made a living being honest, and some made a living not being honest. Booze was a favorite byproduct of the times. Some people got exceedingly rich, and we won't say who, from selling booze on the black market, since it was a forbidden item, and some got exceedingly drunk as a skunk, drinking the stuff. Robbing the rich and giving it to the poor was a fun sort of game, being played by a chosen few. Your history books were much too, too kind to call any names, in fear of being the target of some of the dirty rascals, and besides, they wouldn't get any of the booze if they said anything. However, some of the rascals were so clever about getting and giving, even the cops swiveled their heads to watch the little bugs crawl around different things.

No problem. Lots of families were actually saved by this double-cross of the lawless behavior. Now, how does the author get so smarty about this sort of activity? He lived through most of those times, that's how. And, he saw the KKK help many of the boys in blue shackle the dirtiest of the crum-bums and save a great many poor people from starving. Now, the cops had their hands full trying to control the lawless when the big money was having a ball being mean as ants eating sorghum off the belly of some of their undesirables, yes they did. Big money and lousy politics were the way of life in the great depression. Hmmm hmmm. And it wasn't the KK.K against race, that came later, but can't tell why. Well.....

Fortunately, many men, who belonged to some sort of fraternal organization, were saved by the vows made with their hands on the Bible, and they kept those vows. Nice. Would that the younger men nowadays had that strong integrity. But, you know, integrity has really taken a beating .sometimes. But that's the way the chiggers bite. Some little ragamuffin, remaining nameless, happened to be growing up a little at a time back then. So, when he reached the ripe old age of 17 he hitch hiked to the land of milk and honey, good old California. Woodland, that is. One fine evening he saw a young lady jump from her parked car and rang the door bell for good old Teddy for a nice date. And wouldn't you know, this ragamuffin was charmed silly by this young lady?

Time marches on. At 17, Jim was beginning to take on some semblance of manhood, and got a job as usher showing people to their seats (as if they didn't know where they were already). And in due time, he was fitted with a custom made uniform, that didn't hurt what it hung on at all, and would you believe, that same lady (or girl) got a job in the same theatre "so I could be near you." Now how can a uniform do that sort of magic? My, my. Well, as seniors in high school, both seemed to feel this could turn into something wonderful, as they say. Didn't happen. The boss doorman liked what he saw, and gave our hero the pink slip so he could have clear sailing, so they say. Well.

Wasn't long until our hero dated a girl he met on a tennis court, and after a few nice dates, here and there, she said to this gullible hero, "I think I'm in love." "Yeah? Who with?" "You."

And the farmer hauled another load away. Dumb? Was he ever dumb? What a question. They say, love is a many splendered thing. Sure it is.

Twice dumped. He had to have B.O. or some other unforeseen problem that was mining his love life. "A fine romance" a popular song of the times — not this time, junior. Man, that hurt. Now what's the best thing to do at a time like this? He had rented a room in Del Paso Heights from the most wonderful Italian couple. So. the little Italian lady had the answer. A big dish of Pastachuta. Man, it worked. But that Ain't all. She had heard him bawling when he came home that day and sprawled across the bed, so she cleverly said, "I want you to meet this Diva Will you do it?" Why not? Let's make it three in row, strike out Jim, they call me.

Sunday evening came too soon, but our hero stuck our his chin and marched into the Methodist Church with his landlady and right away, they were ushered to the front row, smack in front of the choir which was singing that most beautiful Christmas song, The Messiah, and who was singing the lead with a voice trained for the San Francisco Opera and a volume that shook the rafters with beauty and music? Now how could you have known? It was our Diva, LaVey Sargent, and she sang straight at Jim. How come? She was tipped off, that's how come.

This was the most beautiful girl Jim had ever seen, and her voice was caressing his heart like nothing else ever had, and — no, it can't be. But after church services, she, and her folks, came straight at Jim, pre-arranged, of course. They stopped just three feet away, and while names and all that good stuff, were being batted around, Jim, not to be outdone, asked LaVey and her cousin, Naomia, if they would like to go for a burger and shake and fries? Oh, yes, indeed, they would. Jim knew deep in his heart, he was in for another dunk in the ice chest. No man on earth can be this lucky. Holy, moly. She was giving Jim a smile that would make the Mona Lisa fall out of her rocking chair.

What to do? What to do? After two great big dumps how could Jim luck out and meet the most gorgeous girl in the world with a voice like an angel, and a smile that made his heart beat like a sledge hammer in the hands of that man who said, "I'll be back"? Well, of course, the answer is simple. Jim has finally flipped his lid, and the little men in white coats will be here any minute. No? It ain't so? This is really true? Jim is really walking this dream to his car and they are on their way to Paradise? It's true, Jim. You must be living right. HEY. She is holding Jim's arm like she likes him. What's going on here? Blood pressure 220, lopressor 82, pulse 230. My, my, my. Jim, you son of a gun. Be sure to say your prayers tonight, Jim. Somebody is looking after you.

23 DEC 1942

CHAPTER 2

The little Italian lady introduced Jim to Mr. And Mrs. Sargent, the proud parents of this Diva, and so our lady retired to her seat to let nature take its course. And it did. The Sargents asked Jim if he would like to sit with them (and you know what? This meeting had all been cooked up. and I'll tell you why..) This might take a while, but it is essential to our story. The Sargents, Mildred and Steve, had been living in fear for 15 years now, afraid their beautiful daughter, LaVey (Steve had brought this pretty name back with him from 'The war to make the world safe for democracy" and when this darling baby girl was born, her name went on the birth certificate, LaVey, and she got her mother's first name for her middle name

As the Sargents hesitatingly remembered the events that brought them up to this point, their thoughts went back to 1925, where the little five year old girls were playing jacks and other games on the sidewalk in front of their home. This was a daily ritual, and the little darlings would hike up their dresses so the bouncing ball would not be impeded while the game was in progress. And it was no different today.

It was also the daily practice of Joe the Punk (as he was called by everyone who knew him) to stand idly by and watch the girls as they played. It had not become obvious to anyone else, but Joe dearly loved to watch the girls hike up their dresses while they played, especially little LaVey. Who unwittingly had the best formed legs, a lovely figure, and the snappiest black eyes apparently passed on to her from Grandma

Hamilton, whose family name was adopted by the U.S. Marine Corps for a base in Southern California.

On this day, Joe had a plan. Diabolic, though it was, he was determined to play it through, since he was half out of his mind with this thought. Joe walked up behind LaVey, caressed her back, and whispered, "Come with me and I'll give you some chocolate candy and some chocolate cookies, all you want. How about it?" LaVey was hungry by now, and Joe knew it, so she said, "OK. You girls go ahead, I'll be right back." And off she went with Joe, hand in hand, to get some delicious chocolate candy.

Instead of going in the front door, as was the custom, Joe took her in the house from the back door. Joe sat LaVey down on the couch, while he got down the jar of chocolate candy. He gave her one small piece of candy and then he went into his act that he had in mind all along.

Unceremoniously he ripped off her dress, and began his evil act of fulfilling his desire by raping this innocent creature to his hearts content, and he did just that. LaVey had cried the whole time with pain, and he just laughed to think he had mastered his desire. But he wasn't finished. No, not Joe. With his hands he ripped her insides as though it was the natural thing for him to do, while poor little LaVey screamed for mercy. But got no mercy from this animal. He just decided to rape her again just for the fun of it, and he did.

Apparently no one could hear from this enclosed room, and Joe was aware of this. So when he had finished his brutal attack, he fell exhausted on top of LaVey, satisfied he had done the manly thing. He looked around, and gleefully saw that blood was splatter everywhere, and that poor little LaVey was covered with blood from head to toe, and that made him the cock of the walk as far as he was concerned.

"Go home," he yelled at LaVey. "I'm pooped.." And brave little thing that she was, she limped out the backdoor and walked as fast as she could next door to her home. By now, the sidewalk games had finished and the other little girls had gone home. She didn't know what to do so she crawled into her little bed and promptly went to sleep.

Sometime later, her mother, who had gone to the store to pick up a few things for dinner, came wearily through the front door, and was frightened out of her mind at all the blood freely splattered all over the front room and tracked right into the little girl's bedroom. She became hysterical and shot into LaVey's bedroom to evaluate what had happened. On seeing LaVey sound asleep, she at first thought the worst, but as LaVey moved when she heard her mother enter her room, she rushed up to the bed and hugged LaVey as though nothing else mattered.

Both talked at the same time, which is normal in situations such as this, but finally the story unfolded fairly straight, enough so that Mildred made the usual precautions of that day, by telling her darling that she must never let anyone know what had happened, as it was the custom for men to shun the girl that this happened to believing she was ruined for life and that society believed it was the girls fault, anyway. And Joe the punk got away scott free..

As the Sargent's sat in church mulling all this over in their minds, tears streamed down their faces, in uncertainty as to what might possibly happen to their daughter, and she, in turn, was singing to the Lord, not knowing she was to meet a handsome stranger, that her folks were sitting by. As the services ended, and the choir leader, Mr. Tipper, congratulated the choir on a magnificent performance, as did everyone else in the congregation, Mildred and Steve, with Jim in tow, tried to get to LaVey amid all this confusion, so they could introduce this good looking guy to their daughter, and say a prayer that their prayers would be answered. And now, here they were, face to face with destiny.

CHAPTER 3

"LaVey, this is the nice young man his landlady was telling us about. His name is Jim Shrum. And this is LaVey, the Diva she wanted you to meet." They both said "hi" at the same time. What was going through LaVey's mind was "Wow. He's good looking. I hope he's not like all the other ego busters." And in his mind, "She sure is beautiful but they are the worst kind. She probably thinks I have a million bucks." But what he said was, "You sure have a good voice. I was amazed that you hit those high notes without any trouble." Mr, Tipper, who was standing right beside her said, "She ought to. She has one of the clearest sopranos I've ever worked with."

As Mr, tipper moved on, He could see that he wasn't the one they were looking at. LaVey's cousin, Naomia, moved in and smiled. There seemed to be a young man sort of hanging around Naomia, so Jim thought maybe things will be alright, alter all. But wait. Jim had been dumped by two brown eyed beauties, and he knew he was on the rebound, so mother of all mothers, here are two more brown eyed beauties standing right in front of him, smiling. To break the awkward silence Jim suggested they go for shakes, and burgers now, and the other guy said "That's a good idea." Sure, it was, thought Jim, if I pick up the tab.

Sitting in the mom and pop restaurant, the waitress automatically handed the bill to Jim, as he missed the cue from the other guy. Well. Thought Jim, there will be other days, but things will be better timed, too. Jim and LaVey kept looking at each other, but so did Naomia look at Jim. Well, now. When they had finished Jim thought he had a good idea. "Look, I'm on the graveyard shift at the base, so, looking straight at the other guy, (no names as yet), "Why don't you take Naomia home and I'll take LaVey home, and go on to work there?"

What could the other guy do? He was stuck and he knew it. But, that was what he wanted in the first place. Now. Things were looking better. As he pulled up in front of LaVey's house, in his old "36 Chevy, he killed the motor, and turned to face LaVey, the brown eyed beauty, but on cue she drew back just a little, and he got the point and that made poor old Jim wonder if he was getting ready to kiss the dust again. No, she just smiled, and began to make small talk, so maybe things will work out after all.

Unbeknownst to both of them her folks had garaged their car in the rear, and were just unside the bedroom door, peeking out to see if there was anything to see, and there wasn't. LaVey had indicated to Jim she didn't kiss on the first date, so he was satisfied for the time being. After a few more minutes of small talk, LaVey said she better be getting in to go to bed, and said, "good night". Then she asked, "if you want to, you can call me, and then we can talk on the phone for a while?"

Jim said he would call. He already had her phone number, so he wasn't too far behind the times. When he got back to his room, Jim called and asked if it would be OK for him to come over and go to church with them next Sunday. If he could have seen through the phone, he would have been very excited, as LaVey was extollimg his merits to her folks a mile a minute. Going to church is always a safe step. Unless the preacher gets too wound up. He didn't know if she had parked right next to the phone but it only rang once. Hmmni hmmm. So far, so good. As the song says, "When will you ever learn". OK, he was willing.

Christmas came with flying colors, music and all. And wouldn't you know, (but Jim didn't) he had moved in on LaVey's emotions. It caught her by surprise, too. She had been looking toward their next meeting quite anxiously. Jim knew instinctively that he could kiss her goodnight next Sunday, and he was ready. Nary a word about Payson, Utah, though Jim thought it would have been proper if LaVey's dad had been given some of the land, instead of his brother getting it all, and this made

LaVey think highly of Jim to say so. It was Steve that had saved the farm, in the first place.

Goodnight kisses were very all right, now, and maybe just a little lingering to go along with it. Week after week, LaVey and Jim were termed a twosome as they went to her church each Sunday, much to the consternation of some of the church boys, who had been trying to date her unsuccessfully, as she held tightly to her morals of no smoking or drinking, and no smut, so this ruled out all but two who would have loved to date her, but they were more like brothers, and she knew that. She dearly wanted to sing in her own church, but a popular quartet squeezed out all others. Other churches were always calling her, and even Jack Matranga had her sing in his radio Catholic Hour, which went over with the public with a bang.

Fraternal organizations took up a lot of her time, especially Jim's Blue Lodge, the Scottish Rite, the Ben Ali Shrine, her own Eastern Star Chapter, Rainbow Chapter, (she was their soloist) but most of all, she loved singing the Jeannette MacDonald-Nelson Eddy songs with husband Jim, now, and took them all over the country and Hawaii, and then she was given an appointment to be the vocalist for the United States Army Band, when Glenn Miller pulled his men out of the band on the coaching of General "Hap" Arnold, who loved to hear her sing, and Miller went to England, so music became the life blood for LaVey and Jim along with M.C. work and other entertainment wherever they went. A very popular duo. But still no calls from her church, but she loved the Lord mightyly.

Their wedding date was December 23, 1942. Jim, usually the Master of Ceremonies on their show business dates, (Showboat, among all the others) would introduce their numbers and say, "LaVey is the Singer, and I just go along for the ride". In truth, he had a very nice voice. They played the Hotel Del Coronado, The Empress Hotel in Canada, the Hilton in Chicago, LA, etc, the Royal Hawaiian, just naming a few. When Jim got the call to go through the chairs in their Eastern Star Chapter, after he had become a Past Master of his Capital City Lodge, then they were really kept busy .While Jim was busy in administration,

LaVey showed her mastery of Biblical people by perfect lectures of Martha and Electa.

CHAPTER 4

Under Good of the Order, the Worthy Matron asked LaVey and Jim if they would be so kind as to show some pictures in the overhead screen and comment on them for the pleasure of those present, and would the Secretary be so kind as to give a briefing in the Newsy Notes for those who could not attend this evening to see the loveliness of the Hawaiian Islands.

"It will be our pleasure", said LaVey, who just delighted in talking about Paradise. "When the huge troop ship slowly pulled into the harbor, the first thing that impressed us was the Aloha Tower, with a large clock on all four sides for the benefit of all to see. You can't miss it. We saw the beautiful palm frees gently swaying back and forth and heard the most beautiful music in creation, teasing our senses along with the delightful and lovely dancing of the hula girls and boys, led by Hilo Hattie. In watching the overhead screen, you will get the feeling that you are there, and that's just what you are supposed to think.

"And then Hilo Hattie steps up to the mike and sings 'Aloha oi' one of the most beautiful songs ever written, to further hook you into the Hawaiian culture, and you will be. It doesn't take long for you to feel like you want to stay here forever, and believe me, your eyes will be misty when you do finally board the plane, or ship, bringing you back to so-called civilization..

"While in Hawaii, you will want to tour the islands, all of them, to take in the unadulterated beauty that God, in all his infinite wisdom, has lovingly made from the ashes of the many volcanoes erupting from the sea. Years have gone by. A must-see is the figure and the final resting place of the first King of the islands, King Kamehameha. Also see the 'upside' down falls on the way up the mountain to the summit and the Pali.

(And all the time the camera kept rolling to accentuate LaVey's narrative, which gave the erie sensation that you were there). "While watching the dancers perform, there will be a wise guy announcer exhorting you, especially the guys, to watch the hands, as they tell the story of the dance..

"After you have taken in all the gorgeous scenery, you will start down the other side of the mountain to the windward side, and you will see 'Rabbit Island' in the sea a short distance from the shore. And don't overlook the Mormon Temple ands the extension of Brigham Young University. a beautiful school. Then take in the various tourists stops, where your guide will ask some visitor to taste poi, ands if you say it tastes like paste, he will say 'I wouldn't know about that. I've never eaten paste'. Just a little fun.

"You will see a 'native' open a coconut with a stationary knife and then he will ask if .any of you want to try it, and someone always does. When we were there, a big, bruising, rawhide cowboy takes the challenge. He hits the coconut with the knife, then with a big rock, and even whacks his wife over the head with it, but no luck. It doesn't break. So he gets so mad, he yanks out a rusty .45 and shoots the coconut right between the eyes, while his mother-in-law was holding it. Good move.

"Then we pass the home of Pat Morita, the TV star, who had his legs straightened as a kid at the Shriner's Hospital for Children. You wouldn't want to say anything bad about the Shriner's in his presence.

"Then you will pass the rain mountains, and next stop, the ARIZONA, semi above the water, protected by topping, for the many men in their permanent grave, administered to by The Lord, Jesus Christ. You will then notice ninety degree salutes from the service men, slowly lowering the salute to it's proper restring place, by their side. And if you have mist in your eyes you won't be alone.

"Then you will pass Pearl Harbor at a very slow pace, in deference to those who gave the supreme sacrifice for you. And now, time to go to your apartment for the rest of the day. Goodbye."

CHAPTER 5

Since LaVey and Tim usually go places together, and since Tim dearly loved to go with LaVey and be with her in her in her Eastern Star work, (she couldn't get a church assignment) he felt obligated to answer the call from Leah Schmidt to be the Worthy Patron during her year as Worthy Matron, and it worked out beautifully, with MarLyn playing the piano as a surprise for Dad, Jim. She was a member, also. as the work of the Star Points was taken straight out of the St. James Bible, which is usually accepted by most Christian churches.

Belonging to the Eastern Star Chapter never deterred the Shrums from their church activities, now being at church whenever the call came. Naomia was curious one day about the pull of the Eastern Stars and Masons on their members, and ask them about it. "LaVey, why are you going to Eastern Star activities and not church activities?" "For the simple reason, the church people don't ask me to do anything for them and the Eastern Star does. I feel I have a talent that God gave me so I want to use it. Does that make sense?" "Yes it does," said Naomia. "And it's the same reason for Tim. He has a number of degrees and talent for leadership, management, and behavioral sciernce and he can't put them to use for the church he loves, so he wants to use them somewhere in a legitimate way, and belonging to the Masons he can help crippled children by his dues to the Shrine, and work with community projects for all sorts of good things." "Oh, that's just wonderful," said Naomia," but aren't Masons a cult or something just as bad?"

"Heavens, no," answered LaVey. "The. St James Bible is always open on the Alter, and they take an oath with their hands on the Bible that they will always honor their mother and father, God, Country, their fellow man, and if they are married, the same oath applies to their spouse and children, and if they don't do that they will be kicked out of the Masons and all other Masonic affiliations. They are very strict about it. More so that a church would be. I guess you could say, they make better men out of good men."

Before Naomia could catch herself, she cried, "Now how come I didn't marry a Mason instead of that so and so that I did marry?" Both got a good laugh our of that. Then LaVey couldn't contain herself any longer when she said, "Jim is starting through the chairs of his Lodge, and that means in time he will be the Master, if he is elected."

"You would have to be the one to marry Tim. I had my eyes on him, too. But look who I married? And divorced, too," wailed Naomia. "There are still lots of good men out there, Na" "Well, if you see one, send him my way," said Naomia. "I don't know about that, Na. Sometimes I have trouble remembering things. Maybe I'm just getting old, as they say." When I take my bath, I always put my rings on the dresser but last night, I couldn't find them this morning, I found them in the kitchen, right where I put them last night. Isn't that awful?"

"Oh that doesn't mean anything. We all do nutty things." "Yeah, I guess your right, Na" "Hey, LaVey, want to go over that song you gotta do in Chapter Wednesday?" "Oh, yes I do. Tim always sings the harmony. He's good at it." "Yes, I know," Na said dryly. She gave LaVey the intro and LaVey started to sing - "Soft as the voice of an Angel, breathing a lesson unheard, Hope, with a gentle persuasion, whispers a comforting word. Then when the night is upon us, why should the heart sink away, Hope for the sunshine tomorrow, After the breaking of day. Whispering Hope, oh, how welcome thy voice, Making my heart, in its sorrow, rejoice."

And then she started to cry. "Oh, Na, what would I do without Tim to sing the harmony? I just have the awfullest feeling he might go to Heaven before I do, and then what will I do for his voice caressing mine?

We've sung duets together since 1942 and I'm so used to his golden (I think so anyway) baritone, I think I would go bust." "Nonsense," said Naomia,

"You have a trained opera voice. You would do just fine."

In a nostalgic tone, LaVey said, "We have several favorites. One is the song made famous by Inglebert. 'Please Release Me'. Another is a little but smaltzy, 'Yours'. 'Yours till the stars have no glory, Yours till the birds fail to sing, Yours to the end of life's story, this pledge to you, dear, I bring, Yours in the gray of December, here or on far distant shores, I've never loved anyone the way I love you, how could I, when I was born to be- Just Yours' And LaVey remembering Jim's love for her, puckered up and cried.

"LaVey, your voice is better then ever before, especially when you are singing to Jim this way. Oh, yes, you did. Don't deny it. It was so obvious, but don't throw it away, either, If only someone would sing to me like that. It is just so wonderful that two people like you and Jim have this special love in your hearts for each other. You are both lucky. If you go to Heaven first, you know Jim will be right by your side. You will never be alone. And if he goes first, you will be right by his side. It is so sweet, only God could make something like this happen" If you need me for anything, LaVey, just let me know.

And in LaVey's mind, she was thinking, .how good, and how pleasant it is to have people like Na as a cousin, and someone like that you can depend on. And going through Na's mind she was wishful thinking, I wish I could find someone like Jim to make me feel the Way LaVey does. about him. She almost worships him. And he with her. As the song says, 'love is a many splendered thing.' And I wish I had a share of it..

LaVey and the Author

CHAPTER 6

As Naomia went back to her regular schedule, LaVey got some shears from the garage and went to work on her pass time, pruning shrubs, and anything else that got in her way. She just loved to work in the yard Naomia noticed LaVey working and it reminded her of the time the buzzard and the rabbit bought a house in the country that was in a run down condition and determined to fix it up, and maybe make a few bucks off of it. It was agreed the rabbit should go into town and get some fertilizer for the dead lawn..

As is the practice with rabbits, he was gone a long time. When he got back, he was amazed at how beautiful the buzzard fixed up the place but the dead lawn was an eye sore. He rattled the front door, but it was locked, so he leaned on the door bell. It was opened by a butler in full regalia. "Where's the buzzard," he yelled at the butler. "Oh, sir, you must mean Mr. BuzZARD. Sir, he's back in the yard." "Well," said the rabbit, "You go tell Mr. BuzZARD

That Mr. RabBIT is here with the fertilizer?"

Na always got a kick out of remembering this one. While she was starting away in her car, LaVey got some shears from the garage and headed for the shrubs. She loved pruning the shrubs, whether or not they needed it, And they usually needed it. Just then, she threw the shears down and ran into the house. She had forgotten to turn off the heat from under the tea kettle and it was whistling Dixie. "Now why," she wondered, "did I put the kettle on to heat? I don't remember, but who cares?"

She just left the shears where she threw them, and by now had completely forgotten them anyway.

Well, it was time for "As the World Turns," so in the easy chair and promptly went to sleep. When she woke up, Tim had just come in the door from the garage, and said, "Why don't we go over some of those songs so we will be in good voice when some one calls and wants some music?" "Oh, no, I don't feel like singing, anyway." Tim had noticed she was getting this way more so all the time, but he couldn't figure out why. "Honey, you know my voice isn't worth a hoot without your voice to lead the way." "Oh, I'm getting so I don't want to sing anyway."

This was not like LaVey at all. She has sung all her life, and has a voice equal or better than that of some of those opera singers, from what we've been told. She doesn't want to go to Chapter any more, and that's not like her. Grouchy? Hardly the word for it. And she loves her church, but lately she doesn't seem to have any interest in it. And she just loves Relief Society, because it helps so many people. She doesn't seem to be sick. What could it be? Bashful? Not a chance. Afraid of crowds? She has been in front of crowds all her life, so that couldn't be it.

OK. Just forget it. It's probably something personal that she doesn't want to talk about. We all have these days. Well, its getting late, so bed, here we come. I love to go to bed early and think over the things we've done that day, to see of we could have done anything different or better. Everything seems to be in order, so time to say my prayers. Where's LaVey? Oh, she's probably fixing her face, or whatever she has to fix. Me, I just jump into bed and hope I hit it square on.

No rest for the wicked. That alarm clock is getting to be a nuisance. Some day I've got to do what I wanted to do to the Army bugler. He was a nice guy though, When six o'clock came around, so did he. As a matter of fact, I used to go on liberty with him before my wife came to join me. I just happened to think of something. My wife told me last night to fix my own breakfast. OK, I can do that. Hey. It just dawned on me. She slept way over on her side of the bed. Why did she do that? We've been married for over 59 years now. In December, it will mark our 60th anniversary. Maybe she's afraid I won't get her a present.

Here she comes for breakfast. I always fix enough for two, so all is in order. Two eggs scrambled and two sausages, just right. "Hi, honey," I tried to be light about it. "How come you slept way over on your side of the bed?" "Oh, I didn't want to wake you when I came to bed." OK. Made sense, Sort of "I thought I'd break the ice by saying, "I thought I'd drive for one of the car companies today. I'm going nuts doin' nothin'" "OK." So off to work we go, just whistlin' while we work' - No, Disney, you don't have to worry.

CHAPTER 7

    MarLyn, ever ready with something to laugh about, or even to pull a joke on some unsuspecting soul, came into the kitchen just then, and said,"Dad, I had a dream last night, and it taught me how to speak in Siamese. Want to learn?" "Why not." This has to be good, It isn't possible to learn a language from a dream. Is it? "OK, shoot." "Now, face the East, hold your tongue with your thumb and forefinger, and repeat after me." This ought to be good, so I did as directed. "Ready? Say, Oh, wha, tay goo Siam." I did exactly as told, and I doubt if I will ever be the same.

    MarLyn nonchalantly walked out of the kitchen still in one piece. LaVey had a big smile on her face and it was worth it just to see that smile again. For the past two years, or so, LaVey just wasn't the same person I married way back in 1942, more beautiful than ever, but not the same personality. I knew these things happen to everyone, almost, since Chad studied all sorts of personalities during my stint with the behavioral scientists. Nothing really earth shaking, but enough change to make me wonder if she was having some sort of behavior invasion that I should know about.

    After breakfast, I kissed my brown eyes beauty and said Gotta go. I'm gonna drive to the city by the bay for a car company." This was always a real hum dinger because of the traffic, and it never gets better. We usually (we travel in a semi caravan) stop somewhere along the way for a break in the nerve department, and it helps. We have to go through the turn styles, as we call them, and give the man the usual two bucks ransom to be reimbursed when we get back. Sometimes the traffic backs up all the way to Vallejo.

From that point on, hold on to your suspenders, as the traffic merges with the traffic coming in from Oakland and and all points East. Lotsa fun. Off to the West is the man-made peninsula with the high rise hotels and fishing fleets. You can have more fun fishing from here than putting itching powder on that little oval just before your wife sits down, or vice versa. It's much better going to San Francisco this way that approaching it from the Golden Gate entrance, and three dollars cheaper, too. But, what the heck. San Francisco is a beautiful and fascinating city no matter how you approach it.

One day, coming back to the Bay bridge, a cab driver motioned me to roll my window down, so I obliged, and he yelled at me, "Hey. You gotta flat - head." And he got a big laugh out of that, so I had to grin, You can't get mad at people for wanting a laugh now and then. And I couldn't get mad at the next turn of events. While I was stopped, a lady, who was on the cell phone, smacked me a good one in the rear, and that always brings one of San Francisco's finest to the scene. Way to go, Joe.

After the usual trade of names, and so forth, the lady said, "if you need any further information, call me at this number, and if my husband answers, hang up." Well... By now, I was wondering how my wife was getting along. She sure was acting strangely at times. I didn't know whether to sing or run around the block. My daughter used to say, "Dad, when you sing with Mom, you sound like a frog burping up flies." There's nothing quite like the compliments you get from your own kids. Well, I love them anyway..

On one trip back to Sacramento, I decided to take a short cut from freeway 80 up 505 to freeway 99. It was dark and I wasn't happy about that anyway. Off to the right was a well manicured cemetery so I stopped to admire its beauty. There was a freshly dug grave nearby, and two cars parked nearby, so I assumed someone was getting some overtime. As I got near, a drunk came spiraling up to take as look, also, and he fell in the grave. I couldn't get to him in time to try to stop him, but no matter, another man was already in the grave, so maybe he could help.

While the drunk was trying to claw his way out of the hole, the second man said, "You can't get out by yourself." But he did. And so it goes. It kinda reminded me of my own father who grew up on a farm, and he can tell you things you wouldn't believe about farm animals. His favorite jackass fell in a deep hole they were digging for a well, and my Dad ran to the farmhouse to get help, and his brother, George, said I know how to do this. So he got a shovel and started filling the hole and make it a burial for the jackass since it was too heavy for them to lift out. As he got the last shovel of dirt in the hole, the jackass blythly walked off the top of the dry dirt. A dumb jackass, or

Back home, Jim grabbed his beautiful wife and kissed her soundly, and told her, "I love you, Honey." This was his favorite expression, and it never did make LaVey mad.

This was what he told LaVey when they first became engaged, and it has since become his favorite salutation on coming home to her.

Upon arriving home, Jim wanted to catch up in the latest news .so he flipped on the TV. The newsman was in the midst of his favorite game of criticizing any and all who were in government, and he picked up with "—and if you want to get your country out of the hole, and a pocket lull of money, just go to war against the United States."

Enough of that, Jim said to himself And he looked over at the coffee table and saw the most prized picture he had, the picture of LaVey and Jim taken by the finest photographer anywhere, Mr, Hollingshead, in Woodland, California. And he prized this dearly. It showed LaVey in all her innocence and beauty. And it showed Jim ... it sure did. While viewing her lovely face, Jim said to himself "I don't want to die.."

He couldn't help but reflect on how they met. Two people, born thousands of miles apart, brought together in church, and destined to meet. He felt that it must have been by the grace of the Almighty, the Supreme Ruler of the Earth, from that House not made with hands, eternal in the Heavens. The meeting of the two was not without the usual catty remarks. 'Oh, she's so beautiful. She must have been meant for me' was directed at Tim. And 'how could he resist? All that beauty thrown in his face.' Even Jim's own relatives thought he must have lost his mind marrying such a beauty. "Now I'll bet he goes high hat."

Tim paid so much attention to LaVey, his own daughter, MarLyn, was curious about his love for her until one day in the funeral home where his father lay in state, we walked out into the hallway, and suddenly my father broke down and cried like a baby after viewing his own father who had gone on to Heaven. "I knew then, that my father loved me, but due to his Cherokee ancestry, it was difficult for him to show it." Yes, my Daddy loves me. Today, I saw my Daddy cry.

Sometimes, young people have a hard time trying to define one thing from another, It falls back on the old technique of problem solving, define the problem (never easy), discover the cause, if you can, and then arrive at a solution, which is enough to make a preacher love his wife. On the way home from driving cars one day, I saw a signboard that said, DO YOU HAVE ALZHEIMER'S DISEASE? Golly, gee. I hope not. It gave a number to call and the people to talk to: The Hospice Program. I remember they had helped when my good friend, LeRoy Cassel, in Woodlamd passed away. They were a tremendous help to his wife, Gracie, a lovely and gracious women. A very nice reminder if anyone should need this help.

By the way, Tim wondered, what causes Alzheimer' s Disease, anyway? Some say if you have lost your memory that shows you might have it. Others say if something happened in your childhood, that would do it. Even the most intellectuals have trouble defining it, or even to tell if you have it. My uncle Fud facetiously says there are more theories as to what causes it as there are chigger bites on the seat of learning.

He told me on day, "Don't procrastinate. That's for lazy people. That's for the ones that don't know how to do first things first Smart people. call that 'prioritizing' but I don't use that word 'cause I can't spell it. This is a little off the subject but don't procrastinate, keep your word remember your values, and for Heaven's sake, don't exaggerate, that causes more trouble than a flea on an elephant.

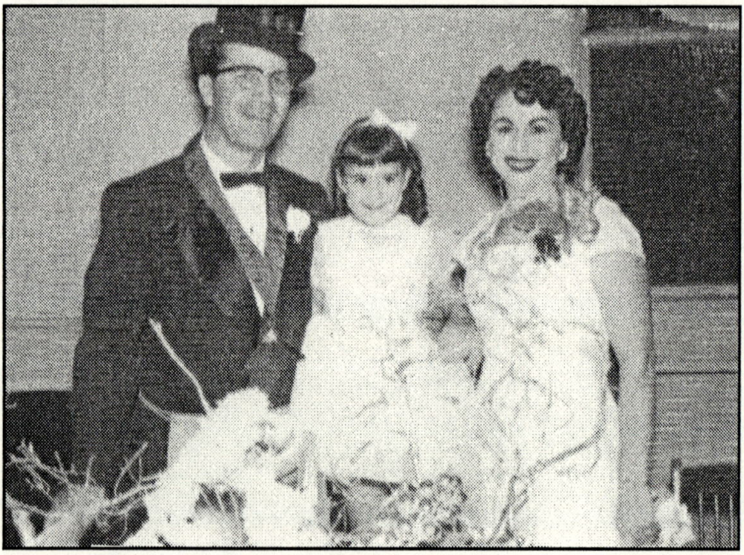

CHAPTER 8

A couple of days later LaVey got a call from Wilma Silvera, the organist for Rainbow Chapter, and also a superior court judge who has a decided desire for all juvenile rapists to be sent to her court. And they, in turn, have a huge desire never to be assigned to her court. Now there must be a reason for all this. And the rapists know better than anyone about their fate. When LaVey picked up the phone, Wilma asked LaVey if she had ever read a book by Henry Wilson Coil, Sr. "No, I haven't," answered LaVey. "Well, let me tell you, that man must stay awake day and night reading past history. He wrote a book called Freemasonry through Six Centuries. And it is a dilly..

"Coil was as distinguished California attorney scholar an author. A Phi Beta Kappa, and graduated cum laude from Colorado College, and the Denver Law School. Quite impressive, isn't it?" "Sure is." "Here are just a few of his jewels. The early development of Freemasonry and its character are unknown. Laws and information were translated orally, and sometimes lost in the their confusion. Until the latter half of the nineteenth century, it was the almost invariable habit of Masonic writers to attribute great antiquity to the craft. The Rev. James Anderson, not only attributed a knowledge of geometry or Masonry, to Adam and to all of the Hebrew patriarchs, and stated that the 'Israelites, at their leaving Egypt, were a whole kingdom of Masons, well instructed, under the conduct of their Grand Master Moses, who often marshall'd them into a regular and general Lodge while in the Wildernes.' Isn't that exciting? Wow. This stuff really goes back in history. And to some great people and great teaching. "I'm right in the middle of this book but I'll clue you in when I finish." "OK."

Just them the phone rang. It was Everett White and he wanted Tim to call him back. So when Tim walked in the door late that day, LaVey had a smile on her face as she told him Ev wanted him to call. She knew. You don't fool the wife all the time, or even some of the time. "Hey, Ev, this is Tim. LaVey said you wanted me to call." "Yeah, I did. Listen, Tim, I'm in a bind. I know you've been coaching candidates for over .two years now, and you know the work forward and backward. The Jr. Steward has just been transferred back East on his job, and I'm short one man in the line. Would you help me out and fill in for me tonight?" "Sure, Ev, glad to do it."

"Yeah, fill in," from LaVey, "what's he gonna do next week? There aren't any other coaches ready to step right in the way you can." "Yeah. Never thought of that." "The heck you didn't. You ought to be more egotistical. You always think everyone else is smarter than you. I know better. Why do you think your military commanders always picked you for the tough jobs? You've got the smarts and if you don't admit it, I will." "Ah, honey, you're just prejudiced." "Sure, I am. But how many officers can remember the work after just one session with a coach?" "Well, Let's just take it one thing at a time."

"Well, Smarty, did you know the other Lodges are considering running you for president of the Sacramento Valley Board of relief?" "No?" "Yes, and as you know, if you get it, you will automatically be the Master of Ceremonies at the spring Breakfast honoring the Superior Court Judge from Los Angeles, the great Joe Shell? All this at Governor's Hall?" Tim just looked like someone had unceremoniously whacked him a good one with a pizza pie. "Hey, wouldn't that be something? To meet an important man like the Judge?" Well, he got the chance. He was elected like his know-it-all wife had said.

He never expected it to happen the way it did. Just before his introduction of the Judge had ended, the judge jumped up, put his arm around Tim's shoulders and said, "Tim just told you who I am and what I do for a living, but I want you to know you have one of the finest men I know and probably the best M.C. anywhere, and if you let him rest on his laurels you're missing a good bet.

When Tim got home, he asked his wife, "Honey, did you hear what that man said about me? I was so flattered I dropped a whole hand full of mashed potatoes." "What? You mean you're still eating peas with a knife?" Smart alec.

What a relief. LaVey was in good mood. "Well, I'm glad you're cavorting with good people." What's that? He's doing what? Why, He's never done that in his life. He is a good, upright citizen. He can be a smart alec, too, you know. But he had sense enough not to say that.

Tim's phone rang then, and that got him off the hook, so to speak. For some silly reason that reminded him of the story that Andy Graves used to tell at his graduation lunches for his management classes. A gentleman went into a bar to wet his whistle, but when he saw the bar was named 'The Noose' he left because he didn't want to hang around. The man apparently had too many because a cop grabbed him by the collar and growled. "I saw you walking down the street with one foot on the sidewalk and one in the gutter, hippety hop. You're drunk." "Whassat?" "I said you're drunk." "Oh, thank you, ossifer, I thought I was crippled for life."

Well.....A truck went by extolling the virtues of calling the Hospice program at the nearest hospital to see if one of your loved ones had a behavior problem that might be taken care of at an early age. Silly man. That's foolish thinking, isn't it? .Now what hospital, or even a doctor, can tell about that sort of thing? It's all in the mind, as it were.

By now, Jim had come to the end of his year as Worshipful Master of Capital City Lodge and it was time to turn over the gavel to the incoming master. He needn't worry. He had a wife that was just full of ideas. When they got home from the installation of the next master, she casually said "Honey, have you given any thought as to what you want to do now?" Now, why should have given any thought as to that? I'm a happy man. I eat regularly, shave when I have to, eat a little too much, 'Dream

Kong With Me' the Perry Como bit running though his mind, he was a happy man. Until.....the phone rang.

"Tim. I need a man to run for Worthy Patron of Rainbow Chapter, with me as Worthy Matron, and your wife can be Electa. Isn't that just great?" All this wonderful talk from Leah Schmidt, the newly elected W.M. And wasn't he thrilled? His wife seemed to think so. She was beaming like a searchlight at sea. So, out of the frying pan into the fire, like they say. And of course, your daughter, MarLyn can play the piano for our specials. Now, why didn't he think of all this before?

CHAPTER 9

Worthy Patron of Rainbow Chapter? And LaVey knows all about this? All that hugging, and kissing, all make believe, and enough to make a preacher love his wife, also? Well, let's take a little thinkin' about this. He just got through eight years of memory work albeit he loved every minute of it. And now not only two more years of memory work but there's a whole lot of chasing around that goes with this. Red Skelton used to have a little program that went something like this. 'If I dood it, I get a whoopin'. I dood it' And he got a whoopin'. OK, Let 'er fly. And he's sure he'll get a whoopin'

"OK. Leah Schmidt, Worthy Matron, I'll take a crack at it. 'Where's the barrel?" Well, things weren't so bad. He was noted for doing good work, that's why Leah wanted him for her patron, and LaVey had already approved the deal, and he knew that, so he went to slaughter with an open mind. After seven years of memory work in the Lodge, here was two more to add to the list. Between Leah's perfect work and Tim's work, together with an excellent program, their years were a resounding success.

And besides, MarLyn played the piano for special occasions, and LaVey and Tim were kept busier than an elephant looking for a flea with their duets of 'My Hero', 'I'll See You Again', "Always', 'Yours', 'Blue Hawaii' and all the favorites of Jeannette McDonald and Nelson Eddy, and a few more besides. Actually, it was a fun two years, but wearing. Then, to make the cheese more binding, they went right into the

Choraleers for more singing. Well, they were classified as professionals, so why not?

And all the time, the two lovebirds would sing these love songs to each other while performing, and that just made it all the better, especially, knowing the two really loved one another.

What a story these two actually made. Born thousands of miles apart, and brought together in church on a fluke circumstance? And then later traveling all over singing for any organization that said the magic words? And to top it all off they were both matinee idols if there ever was one? Was entertaining all over creation their missions in life? Could be. We all have missions, if we would just think about it.

Tim says his mission is also to take care of LaVey ands then some. What a wonderful open mind he has. Would that all men and women listen to their missions. What a wonderful world that would be? There is so much sex attached to love nowadays that you never know which is real and which is not. There was a time you could not even say the word 'sex' without it having a derogatory meaning. There was a real stigma attached to it. Now, it's Katy bar the door.

As the group started to leave the Temple, Wilma asked how Jim was doing? She heard he had a bad virus, "Did he really lose his sense of smell?" "Well, he did at first but he still doesn't smell so good." OK, LaVey you go to bed with the chickens tonight," from Jim. "I called for a doctor's appointment but we can't get one for three weeks. By then, Tim will either be well or dead."

Just as they were getting into their car Klay Stubbs and his wife walked by and said, "Hello," and shot the breeze a few minutes and went on to get their car. LaVey turned to Wilma and said, "If you ever have any electrical problems, Klay is the guy to call. That man is great and he is honest. You don't find that combination very often, anymore. And besides he inherited his mother's smile, Joyce, a beautiful woman."

As they pulled out from the curb, a smart alec yelled at Wilma, "You're a stinkin' judge, and I hate your guts." I never phased Wilma. "Its my court and I'll run it anyway way I please. By the way. When is your case coming to trial?" Wilma turned to LaVey and asked "I heard your Dad and Ewing Walker used to gear their men on by yelling, "over the top with the best of luck and give 'em hell. That's cute. I like it. Did your Dad ever tell you about that?" "He told us about a lot of things after we got him relaxed, but some of them we can't talk about. They make us blush."

Worshipful Master, JAMES D. SHRUM, Capital City Lodge No. 499. F & A M 1969

When General Pershing heard about this cry, he wanted to see for himself just how it affected his men. So he went to the front, unnoticed by Steve and Ewing, and right in front of him, Steve yelled "Over the top, you bastards, with the best of luck, and give 'em hell." And they did. And Gen. Pershing not only gave them the Silver Star, he gave them a star in their crown, which was a mythical star to be given to them by Jesus.

When Kaiser Wilhelm heard about this, a corporal asked him if he was going to do the same thing? His answer cannot be printed. As he turned to retreat something with an awful smell fell from his pants leg. "Well, as Walter Cronkite (spelling?) would say, "And that's the way was, that day, in the slit trenches in France."

CHAPTER 10

Question of the day, did Ben Franlkin's wife really tell him to go fly a kite?

That must have been some meeting at the last Eastern Star meeting,

Wilma called LaVey and said she had the goofiest dream, She dreamed some smart alec got smart with her in court, and her eyes got hot as coals, and she snorted like the winds of a hurricane, and her voice sounded like a rusty foghorn gone berserk and she wiggled in her big chair like the seven year itch in all its glory, and she bellowed at the accused rapist, "Shut up and sit down or the devil's imps will be sitting on your carcass before you see the light of day again. Now," sweetly as if propelled by a mad dog, "would you like to take issue with me again, or would you like to live a while longer without your head having knots on it made by the design of a bed pan?"

Recognizing that agreeing with the court was the better part of valor, he trembled as he said, "Your Honor, I will do exactly as you say." "Your darn tootin' you will". Listen, that Judge Wilma will take any of them on, and she does, She must be from Texas, 'cause you don't mess with a Texan. That's some dream.

"Now, Wilma, let me tell you my dream. As they say, one good turn deserves another, as they say. In my dream we were invited to sing in Governor's Hall for some dignitaries, especially for the installation of the governor, and for the occasion LaVey wanted to sing 'Yours' for it is a love song and one of our favorites. As we sang, Tim thought I was squeezing his hand and giving him that come hither look, as if to say, Let me sing to you, And he nodded and returned that loving look, while I sang- 'yours till the birds fail to sing, yours to the end of life's story, this pledge to you dear, I bring, yours till the gray of December, here or on far distant shores, I've never loved anyone the way I love you, how could I, when I was born to be, Just Yours. I looked down at his peaceful countenance, and I just had to yell at him, "Get up, you lazy bum. You've slept long enough."

MarLyn came in the bedroom just then, took one look at Tim, and asked. "Dad, why are you crying?" And she reached down and took the 8 by 10 picture from his crossed arms, and saw a picture of them being married by Bishop Steinagel.

But make no mistake about it. These two are more devoted to each now that ever. Little jokes never hurt anyone. And Jim could take a joke with the best of them. He just gets sentimental at times. And that endures him to LaVey all the more. "Hey. Mom aren't you going to get the groceries today," asked MarLyn. "Oh, I suppose we had better if we want something to eat over the week end." So off they went in MarLyn's car to gather in some grub. When they came back, they were busy putting the groceries away, when LaVey walked into the family room and said, "Hey, there's a baby on the coffee table"

Tim and MarLyn came to an absolute stop, and then looked at each other. And then continued puffing away the groceries. When Tim got a chance, he went back to MarLyn's room ands asked, "Do you think Mama has Alzheimer's Disease?" MarLyn couldn't talk, she just nodded her head. "Hey. There's some kids playing out in the front yard. I'd better tell them not to trample the flowers," heartbreaking as it is they knew now they were going to lose the most precious person in the world to them. Thunder couldn't have been more clearer or louder than what they had just heard and saw coming from the mouth of the most loving and beautiful women on earth. Tim's head was reeling. MarLyn went into her room and was silently crying..

ALZHEIMER'S DISEASE. The most dreaded and feared disease on earth had just entered into the lives of the most unsuspecting family in existence. How could such a thing happen to LaVey? Sweet, loving, loyal, true, possessed of a great singing voice which has thrilled thousands of people all over the United States, Canada, Hawaii, Mexico, the United States Army Band after Glenn Miller was called to England, and various churches, the Catholic Hour of Jack Matranga, Many Masonic functions and even the Mormon Church in Hawaii on many, many lovely occasions, and now this beautiful voice has been stilled forever.

The first thing Tim did was to call their family doctor at the hospital, for an appointment as soon as they would give it. This was going to take a fight, and that fight had already started. MarLyn was quieter now than she had ever been. What could she do? What could anyone do? With this dreaded disease, there was no return. You knew what, but you didn't know when. The number of your days was with God.

This happened about six months ago from this moment, so they knew there wasn't much time for them to get things in order, and prepare for the inevitable. It is unthinkable that this talented and beautiful woman has received the call to go home to her Father. When finally we got the call to bring her to the hospital for an examination by Dr. Johnson, he was very kind and said she would probably pass away with her heart problem before this could get worse, as he felt that she was in the initial stages of the disease..

CHAPTER 11

She certainly looks her normal self No way would you suspect anything was wrong. But underneath that beautiful exterior lies a mind that has been tampered with that is contrary to that which was designed by her Maker. How did all this happen? At the present time, no one knows. Going back a few years, to update our thoughts, LaVey first saw the light of day on 8 Feb 1922 in the quiet little town of Payson, Utah, Not much happening here, except the little girls playing jacks and other games on the sidewalk in front of their homes.

Occasionally, the bouncing ball would bounce in the street, and one of the girls would run after it without thinking to look for cars, but then there weren't many cars to look out for. When she was delivered, the town's old drunken doctor did the duty and fortunately all went well. One day, when LaVey was about four or five at most, the neighborhood punk enticed LaVey into his house, while his mother was working, and not only raped her, but molested her so badly her organs were left bleeding all over the place.

That enough? While still a child she was kidnapped but managed to escape. And, later she and another girl were accidentally locked in the trunk of a car. More. Her father, Steve Sargent, had his back shot to pieces by a hand grenade in WWI.

Normally, you would think she could not bear children, but she did. Had lots of problems, though. Later. she had three miscarriages. Finally after her son, Jim, Jr was ten-years-old, she had a lovely bouncing baby girl, MarLyn. She had to do most of the work raising the two children, as her husband was on the road for an insurance company.

She never cared much for football, but when Steve Young played, she was right there. She never cared much for Shaq. While at a Shrine social with husband, Jim, she picked off the tray what she thought was a nice big glass of tomato juice. And was she ever happy for a while?

She loved animals, but told MarLyn she should not have brought home that cute little puppy, Princess. But when Princess put her arms around LaVey's neck and kissed her, it was love at first kiss. For both of them. One day, when she was invited to come to Hawaii to be with her Navy Husband Jim, she got seasick so badly the Navy saved a lot of money on food. And when they returned, they decided to take a little excursion up the coast, and was gone overnight. But using a portable cot, they were able to stay the night in a nice patch of poison oak.

Not to be outdone by anyone, LaVey wanted to learn to drive their brand new Buick, so Tim obliged by letting her get on a freeway just south of Lodi, since the traffic was almost nonexistent. Luckily, a highway patrol man she dated once, was waiting near Lodi for those who didn't wish to drive within the limits. He noticed that Tim was having a hard time turning off the switch as they passed him on Main Street going 70 miles an hour. He still laughs about it.

She did have a remarkable sphere of influence. Bringing her husband into her church started the whole thing. This led to two children, a son and a daughter. The son brought in a wife and four children and four grand children. The daughter brought in a husband that couldn't handle a marriage. Then daughter MarLyn, began working in the Oakland Temple doing work for those that passed on through the Pearly Gates.

While in Hawaii, you never want to leave there with out a trip to see and dance with Hilo Hattie at the Royal Hawaiian, or wherever she was playing. It was a real delight.

CHAPTER 12

December 20. The nurses from Hospice do not understand how this brown eyed beauty has stayed this long even though she refuses food or any form of liquid But that does not deter them from their mission, that of making Lavey as comfortable as possible under the circumstances. From time to time they ask Tim to move from his easy chair so they can give her a sponge bath, or some other form of comforting. By now, Tim is in such a state of mind, that he has moved his easy chair over right next to the hospital bed that the Hospice ladies have brought in, together with oxygen, a wheel chair and other necessaries for LaVey's com fort with her hospital bed. The end is obvious, now, but Tim and MarLyn are so loving they cannot tear themselves away from her for any length of time, and the Hospice nurses are so good, they never complain.

Looking back into the life of this classic beauty, she is only 3 days from her 80th anniversary; but the ages have been good to her. Payson, Utah was a quiet little town on February 8, 1922, until the drunken doctor delivered an eight pound screamer that brought a big smile to the tear laden face of Mildred Sargent, and father Steve, who didn't know what to do with his hand-wringing time. What lungs.; they must have jarred the neighbors around them. But they were all friends, and offered all the help for free that was necessary. For the welfare of this fine mother and now her little bit of Heaven, that surely came from the Almighty.

Now, the little one had to be named. Since the drunken doctor couldn't see well enough to write the name properly, the local Bishop took down the name from Steve, who brought it back from France, following WWI, It was LaVey, and middle named after her mother, Mildred. And this was the baby that was destined to do many great things. A great tap dancer, a voice that reached all the way to stardom with the San Francisco opera and starring in many high school and community musicals, and this is just to name a few things.

Romance? Oh, yes. Very popular with the boys in high school and her church. Some would get very angry is she wouldn't date them but she had her priorities — no smoking, no drinking, no swearing and some got so frustrated they said she would not allow them to breath, either. However, her demands were only a few. She was a good Christian girl, and was determined to stay that way. By this time, her folks had moved to Sacramento, where the atmosphere was kinder to Mildred's asthma.

Yes, romance. It can be kind, and it can be cruel. It depends on which way you wish to go. Dates? Oh, yes, lots of dates. But rings? She didn't love any of the dates, but romance was just around the corner. Mrs. Gera, the landlady where Jim had a room, wanted him to meet this Diva, as she had the lead in the Christmas musical, The Messiah Jim had just been dumped by two successive brown eyed beauties, so he knew something was wrong with him, and who wants a loser, anyway? He knew he was safe.

But he was yet to meet this Diva, wasn't he? Love? Never, Romance? Never. Anything more than just, hello, how are you? Nice to meet you. Goodbye. That was it. He knew it, So get in there, Clark Gable, and show them who's who. Yeah. That's the spirit.

"Oh, Jim, this way." Jim had started to go the wrong way when they got to church, so Mrs. Gera steered him to a seat right in front of the choir, where Mr. Tipper was busy arranging the members in their proper places, in preparation for their rendition of the best known Christmas musical of all time. "Good Heavens" Jim couldn't help but exclaim. Right smack in front of him in the choir was the most beautiful creature he had ever seen in his life. And was Mrs. Gera enjoying this? She had a smile that stretched from one ear to the other.

And then they began to sing. Jim couldn't take his eyes off of this beautiful girl from Paradise, and she could sing like an Angel, too. Now, this was too much. It can't be. And Mrs. Gera wanted him to meet this beauty? Why? Had the boys in Sacramento all gone blind, and deaf; too? Something had to be wrong. Here he was a throw away, and he was to meet this most beautiful girl in the world? He's having a dream, that's what. But when he shook his head, and opened his eyes, nothing had changed.

Two hours later, after being mesmerized, he was still in command of his senses. Mrs. Gera introduced Jim to the Sargent family; Steve, Mildred the mother, and the sweetest thing this side of Heaven, and Jim was meeting her. There was only one thing to do now. Don't let her get away. Say something. Anything. Pull your hair out by it's roots, anything. This is just too much. But, no. Everything seemed to be normal. "How about a hamburger and milkshake?" Now wasn't that earthshaking? Well, it was better than a jab in the eye with a sharp stick. And the earth must have shook, for LaVey said, "I am starved, Let's go."

Needless to say, one thing led to another, and they were engaged six months later. Can you imagine that? Jim was engaged to a dream? She doesn't smoke, doesn't drink, doesn't cuss like a sailor, doesn't flirt, goodness sakes alive, what has he gotten into? Married on December 23rd, for real, by Bishop Herman Steinagel, who gave Jim a clean bill of health, along with a little Cherokee blood flowing through his veins. Jim was a big spender. He gave the Bishop two whole dollars, as was the custom at the time.

It seems incongruous looking back at a time like this to the early start of this twosome, to the finer things in life that was theirs? Here she was, the mother of a son and daughter, the grandmother of four, the great grandmother of two, and now destined to go home to her Heavenly Father? How lives do change, and when you least expect it.

She had been so active in the Eastern Star, having been a star point three times teaching the candidates stories of Martha, Ada, Ruth, Esther, and the combination point, Electa, probably the most beautiful of all, and wishing all the time she could have an appointment in church to show her teaching abilities. She had one of the most active and dedicated minds in the teaching profession, and without a credentialed paper in her arsenal of love? And, all the time, Jim lay in his easy chair holding her hand and whispering, "I love you, Honey" whether she could hear or not, made no difference. Love is love, day or night, and it never changed.

Jim knew his time was getting late, but they had made a vow that if one was going home, the other would stay right with that one, so that the one going Home would not be lonesome And every so often, Jim would say, "I'm right here, Honey, and I'm holding your arm, so you are not alone. I love you, Honey, and I'll always be with you either here or in Eternity where the Supreme Ruler of the Universe forever presides. We were married for time and all Eternity, so you will never be alone. Goodnight, Sweetheart."

And Jim fell asleep with exhaustion.

CHAPTER 13

December 21. Whew. Jim just sat there shaking his head and one of the Hospice nurses asked him if he had a headache and he said, "No, but I sure had a weird dream. I dreamed LaVey had gone to Heaven, and as she went through the Pearly Gates her mother met her and asked her if she remembered being told not to tell anyone about being raped. She replied that she remembered, and then her mother said that she had been wrong, because she didn't just get a good husband, she got the best. What a relief.

Probably one of the main reasons her mother wanted her to keep it quiet, was the fact a very ugly stigma was attached to the very word. You were not even allowed to say the word for fear someone would make something of it that wasn't there.

In the early twenties, and even later, many words were considered a no-no even unto themselves. How education has changed the world.

Behavioral science raised it's educated head. For example, Procrastination crept into our language with a meaning that you were putting off until tomorrow what you should do today

Putting it simply, if it should be done, do it now. If you don't do it now, your boss will unwittingly say "You are a slow worker." Slow, because he wanted it done now, instead of later. Keeping your word — was also high on the list, as was knowing your values, and priorities, and for heavens sake, don't exaggerate. The old timers called that -making a mountain out of a mole hill. Alzheimer's disease was not even thought of then, you were just getting senile.-

Bob Bertanelli and Jim, 2nd drove up to the house just then to see how Jim's mother was getting along. They saw a man sitting in his car in front of the house, and Bob, always on the lookout for interlopers, walked up to the car and motioned for the man to roll his window down! The man refused. Now, you don't do that to Bob, because life is too short. He pulled his gun out of its holster and made the request again. This time the man complied, and asked Bob what he wanted, so Bob showed him his ID and asked in a sarcastic way. if the man thought that was enough.

The man pulled out his wallet, and showed Bob a United States Badge, and an ID that simply said, UNITED STATES SECRET AGENT and was, signed by the President of the United States. That's all. Nothing else. By now, Jim, Bob's partner recognized the man, and said, "Bob, this man and I worked together during the Viet Nam War. Our names are not given and we can tell you very little else

The man did relent just a little bit. He said, "I'm not watching your place, That's just a cover. I see my man right over there, coming down the other side of the street, so you two cover me and make sure this collar goes without incident. OK?" "OK." When the man saw he was outnumbered, he did exactly what he was told, and was taken into custody without further action.

Afterward, Bob exclaimed, "Good gosh to Moses, May your armpits be infested with fleas forever, holy mother of Pretty Boy Floyd, surprise, surprise. What next?" "Sorry, Bob, you know I couldn't tell you ahead if time, or I would have."

Afterward, Bob said," I didn't know you were federal." Jim said, "Now, I'm not, but once you're cleared Top Secret, you remain that way until shown otherwise." "Good gosh to Moses," exclaimed Bob. "What will happen next? Holy Geehosofat. Mama mia." "What did you tell that agent," asked Jim? "Oh, nothin' much," answered Bob. "I just showed him the ugliest .38 Police Special hollow point that man can make, and he became my friend."

JAMES D. SHRUM, Worthy Patron, OES
With wife, LaVey and Daughter, MarLyn

CHAPTER 14

December 22. By now, Jim is half out of his mind with grief and worry. He is well aware of the circumstances surrounding Alzheimer's patients. He knows that the experts hold little regard for the conventions attributed to Alzheimer's and the types of aid submitted for use by those who profess to know the most. He doesn't turn down any aid or suggestion in trying to make his wife more comfortable. As a Christian man, he does believe with all his heart that God is the Supreme Master, and that He is calling for those who become "weary" to come Home.

There is no question that LaVey is "weary" and the nurses from Hospice have been almost begging him to tell her that he is willing to let her go Home, but when they do, he gives them that beaten-dog look, and with misty eyes, he begs them to let him keep her just a little bit longer? "What will I do without her? She is everything to me. We do everything together, and go everywhere together. We have always been a team. I always have talked everything over with her, and now I won't have anyone to talk with, or do things with? I just love her with all my heart, and now I'm losing her and I don't know what I can do about it"

He continues with, "Tomorrow will be out 60th wedding anniversary, and I can remember our wedding just as though it happened yesterday. She was so beautiful, and vibrant, and full of life. And now, I have to watch her die a little bit each day. She must be an Angel here on earth. In my heart, I can almost hear that beautiful church hymn. inviting those who are weary to come home. 'Softly and tenderly Jesus is calling, Calling for you and for me, See, on the portals, He's waiting and watching,

Watching for you and for me. Come home, come home, Ye who are weary come home, Earnestly, Tenderly, Jesus is calling, Calling, O Angel, come Home,' And with a pitiful little smile Jim looked up at the nurse and whispered, I just changed the word 'sinner' to Angel." And he hung his head, and tenderly kissed her forehead and whispered, "I love you, Honey," And he hung his head down farther and tried to hide his tears, but they came anyway..

The nurse laid her hand on Jim's shoulder and said softly, "I have another patient to see, so if you don't mind, I'll check on her, but you call me if you need me?" Jim just nodded, and silently thanked her.

Why did I get into this type of work, the nurse silently asked herself? But she knew why, and she wouldn't give it up for anything. Those Hospice nurses are so highly trained, they seemed to know just the right thing to say or do. Those home care givers would call the Hospice nurses constantly if they only knew how to get them, That information is listed in the bibliography. And. there is no charge, but remembrances are always appreciated.

The doorbell rang just then, and it was the telegraph man with a telegram. After Jim read, he put it in his shirt pocket, and went back to his vigil by his wife's side. Her breathing was shallow, now, and he knew that the end was near. Poor LaVey. She won't be able to sing in the Messiah for the Methodist church again, nor will she be able to sing with the U.S. Army band again, no more songs for President Reagan or Nancy again, no more replacement for Glenn Miller to please Gen. Hap Arnold, no more singing for the troops, no traveling to Hawaii to do the Hilo Hattie show, no singing in the church choir, no more Eastern Star or Masonic Musicals, no singing on Jack Matranga's Catholic Hour, no more singing the Jeannette McDonald — Nelson Eddy duets with her husband, (and that hurt), but on the plus side, there must be singing in Heaven for those with the talent.

Would there be any Hollywood productions in Heaven by the Great Producer/director, Myron Hamm, there just had to be? And what about the World Renown Mormon Tabernacle Choir she was invited to sing with? Her voice was one of the standouts of the choir.

LaVey

In her will, she invited Bonnie Grover to sing two songs for her, and one was her favorite, 'In the Garden' that heart-wrenching hymn that invited the weary to walk with the Master: And as they walked across the way, they could see the old rugged cross, where Jesus gave his life for the weary traveler here on earth. But, now, all Jim could do was hold on to LaVey's arm, which was getting colder each day, and watch her leave his love, a little bit each day, and now, it was almost gone.

The nurse had returned earlier than expected and walked over to place her hand on his shoulder to let him know she was with him, Jim reached up and put his hand on hers, thanking her for returning sooner.

He looked up at the nurse, and said, "I never told you this sooner, but last night, even though she can't talk anymore, she woke me up and whispered, "I don't want to die," and she lay back her head, and closed her eyes and I think she has gone to Heaven. Could you check and see if she is OK?"

Today is 27 December 2002. Minutes were precious now.

The nurse was so flabbergasted, all she could do was nod. Then she said to Jim in a tender voice barely audible, with her hand on his shoulder for consolation, "She's gone," Jim asked with misty eyes, "Can you check her pulse, she may have a weak one?" "She's gone." "Can you check her heart? It might still have a weak beat?" "She's gone."

Jim just couldn't believe his wife of 60 years, the mother of his two wonderful children and his only true love, his sweetheart, has gone Home. Jesus had just Softly and Tenderly called her Home. And Jim cried.

Jim had lost all track of time. No food, nor drink, and the date had changed to 3 p.m., 27 Dec 2002. Their anniversary had come and gone and Jim had missed it. He had been so engrossed with having as much time with his wife, LaVey, as he could before he had to do as His Master had wanted him to do. Let her come Home. It was a difficult day that day. The nurse had been softly advising Jim that LaVey only had minutes to live, "so give her your love, and tell her that you are going to do what God has ordained, you are still married to the sweetest girl on earth." "And as Jim heard Him whisper to him, 'Let Her Come home.' Jim kissed her on her brow, and tenderly kissed her lips, and whispered to his sweetheart, "As the Father has asked, I release you and let you go home. God bless you," And Jim sobbed, deep down heart-wrenching sobs, and laid his head down on the lifeless breast of his wife and his eternal love.

He didn't look forward to her services but he knew he had to hold up for the last time he would be able to see is beloved. And this will be on 2 January 2003.

CHAPTER 15

Jim is practically beside himself. How will he handle himself at LaVey's last services? He didn't know. He always thought of himself as strong, strong willed, strong character, strong in everything, and people would come to him for his strength of character to help them through a tough time.

He was mulling over the twx that was sent simultaneously to the DA and Chief asking for exclusive rights to the story that hit national news about their trip to Payson and the results from it, plus all the personal stuff thrown in. The initial fee offered by the Hollywood studio was $33,000,000 to the studio, $100,000 each to the chief and DA for the benefit of their departments only, and $10,000 each to Jim and Bob for their wear and tear of

Well, now, thought the DA, if this themselves and their personal lives, and this was from a lesser studio, maybe one of the big boys might want to increase the ante just a little bit, or maybe a big bit. Let's wait and see. So, the waiting game began.

And the chief began to sing that little ditty to himself, "And the farmer hauled another load away," And coming up the hard way, he was good at this, The chief looked at some of his notes he had been making as the case progressed — On December 20th, LaVey told Jim and MarLyn that a neighborhood punk, (and she was vague about his name, but
it can't be used anyway until the case goes to court), had been friendly with them for a long time so they took him to be a friend. And it had not

come as a complete surprise that he offered to give candy and milk to one of them. "So he took me by the hand, and I thought that was nice of him, and led me into his house by the back door, explaining they always locked the front door to keep out robbers.

"When he didn't go get the cookies and milk right away, I began to get scared, and I asked him about that. So he said in good time. Then he came over and pulled my dress off and pulled off my panties and he put something in me that hurt a lot. I cried but he kept it up. After a while, he slowed down and then he really began to hurt me there and I screamed but he kept it up until he fell down tired. Then he said he had to go to the bathroom and for me to stay put."

"Just as soon as he shut the bathroom door, I ran out of the house and went home and got into bed. And there was blood all over me and all over our floor and all over my bed. I was really scared. I thought I was gonna die."

This was the umpteenth time he had read those notes, but he wanted then etched in his mind so he could use them if need be.

Then he gave his attention to the TWX and all that money and began to smile. He was an honest man but face it, money is money. And the DA felt about the same way. So after a meeting with Bob and Jim, The Chief and DA felt on saver grounds about asking for more money — for their departments, of course. They gave the other studios 48 hours to come up with a better deal, and they were close, but studios do talk to each other, no matter what you hear.

So the original contract was signed, and notarized, and approved by the municipal court so the studio got into action right now to beat the competition They contracted with the national network for exclusive rights and almost twice what they had told the Chief and DA. Well, you live and learn. The program was ballyhood so expertly their percentage was almost 60% of the viewing audience.

And they made a pretty penny off of the deal. To keep good relationships with the city of Santa Rosa, the studio put $100,000 in the Mayor's kitty "for administrative purposes." Sure they did.

Something that the chief and DA held back from the press thinking it wasn't any of their business. At one point in the care giving process, LaVey told Jim flat out that she wouldn't let him show any affection for her because she felt that he was the one that raped her. For the past six months, she wouldn't let Jim near her, and for that reason, she didn't know who he was, but she didn't have any control on his being in the same house with her. To her, he didn't seem like a bad guy, but she didn't think he was her husband. At bedtime, she let him put his hand on her arm because it gave her a sense of security. All this — in the chief's personal report on LaVey's condition.

Just days before LaVey was deprived of her ability to talk, we were both feeling in a good mood, and we started to sing that popular song made famous by Inglbert Humperdink, "Please Release Me" as we had sung duets together for well over 40 years, so we sang. "Please release me, let me go, I don't love you anymore, to live a lie would be a sin, so release me, and let me love again." So I released her and then I silently cried, for I could never release her. And I know she felt the same way until the dreaded disease, Alzheimer's, took over her mind.

As the attendants were preparing the casket with its precious cargo, Jim was standing about five feet from it, and in his heart he was singing one of their favorite songs "Yours till the stars have no glory, yours trill the birds fail so sing, yours to the end of life's story, this pledge to you dear, I bring, yours in the gray of December, here or on far distant shore, I've never loved anyone the way I love you, how could I, when I was born to be just YOURS." Bob and Jim had been watching him to see how he was holding up, and this did it. He began to sob, deep down, heart wrenching sobs, and started to crumble, but Bob caught him just in time, and held him in a mighty hug until he could stand by himself with only a whimper left while LaVey was on her last ride, and he whispered, "I love you, Honey." And LaVey went home.

BIBLIOGRAPHY

The Hospice Program

Most Medical Facilities.

The Alzheimer's Assn.

Golden Page

Del Oro Caregiver Resourc

Primose

Alzheimer Advocacy

Bowen Therapy

Understanding Alzheimer's Disease

The Palms

Mark John Crews and Associates

Living

Marriott

Kaiser Hospitals